ON THE TRAIL OF THE *WINDWARD*

# ON THE TRAIL
# OF THE *WINDWARD*

## A Story of the Norfolk Broads

*BY*

MORGAN DERHAM

*ILLUSTRATIONS BY L. F. LUPTON*

C . S . S . M .

5 Wigmore Street, London, W.1

FIRST PUBLISHED 1948
SECOND IMPRESSION 1950

MADE AND PRINTED IN ENGLAND BY PAGE & THOMAS, LTD.,
SHERATON STREET, LONDON, W.I, AND AT CHESHAM

# CONTENTS

To H.R.F., who first
introduced me to the twin delights
of steering a tandem and
handling a yacht.

*Note to the Reader:* A diagram, showing details of the rigging and lay-out of a typical Broads yacht will be found on page 22. This will help you to follow the descriptions of sailing.

## Chapter 1

### VIKING MOVES OFF

" THERE'S the signboard ! 'Rumsey and Son, Boatbuilders and Yacht-Owners'— that's the place, John ! "

" You're right, Hugh.  Come on ; let's sprint the last hundred yards.  We may as well appear fresh, even if we don't feel it."

" Right-ho ; hold everything ! "

The sleekly-built tandem swayed a little as the two muscular eighteen-year-olds strained at the pedals, seemingly intent on pushing them clean off the cranks.  They had just worked up quite an effective sprint when John Wilson, the curly-haired, cheerful-looking steersman, stopped pedalling and pulled hard on the brakes, swinging the machine skilfully into the rough-surfaced approach to the boatyard.  He brought the tandem to a neat standstill outside the little office, held it upright whilst the back partner, Hugh Rogerson, leapt off, and then swung his leg deftly over the handlebars, and leaned the machine against the boatyard wall.

A sunburnt man in a blue jersey came out of the little office, and said, smilingly, " Good afternoon, gentlemen ; you're for the *Viking*, I suppose ; we've only one other craft out this week, and she's gone already."

" Yes," said John. " Sorry we're a bit late, but we've had a long ride, and the wind hasn't been very kind to us. Still, we shan't mind the wind for the next fortnight ; the more the merrier, once we get afloat ! "

" You'll get plenty of wind, I think ; it's late in the season, and I've never heard of anyone being becalmed in October up here ! "

" We'd better get on board as soon as possible," said Hugh. " We don't want to stay in the boat-yard all night, and there's plenty to unpack and sort out. Have the provisions arrived ? "

" Yes," replied the yard manager, " I think everything is here. Come along with me, and I'll show you where to park the tandem."

He led them round the back of the boat-house, across a shaky wooden bridge spanning one of the many dykes which cut through the yard, and into an empty corner of a smaller shed, which smelt strongly of hemp and tar, and where masts and rigging were laid along brackets on the side wall.

John and Hugh soon took the haversacks off the carrier of their machine, and eagerly followed their guide as he took them to a deeper dyke, which led straight out into the main stream of the River Bure, and against the side of which was moored their home-to-be for the next fortnight, the handsome yacht, *Viking*.

After they had dumped their bags in her well, John went back to the office to complete the necessary arrangements with the yard manager, while Hugh busied himself investigating the contents of the lockers which ran round the side of the well, and giving the cabin a preliminary survey.

" She's well fitted, all right, John," he said, as his friend returned, carrying the large can of paraffin which had been left for them at the office. " The cabin is very roomy, there's nearly enough room even for your long legs! Seems to have plenty of cooking equipment, too ; they've thrown in an extra primus stove ; must have heard from someone about your appetite ! "

" You shall pay for that, my friend ; you know we haven't time to stop and square the account! You sort the lockers out and unpack the grub, and I'll go back and fetch the suitcases from the shed ; don't eat all the biscuits ! "

Hugh carefully sorted out the various packages of food, tucked them away in the lockers, and had a primus stove warming up by the time John returned, struggling with two heavy cases.

" Demonstration of ' Primus-lighting-without-tears ', by Hugh Rogerson ; stand back, everybody, and get ready to duck ! " cried John, mockingly, as his friend bent over the flaring stove.

" All a primus needs is a little understanding," replied Hugh. " That's why you'll never light one properly ! Just watch this, and see for yourself how easy it is. You simply let the meths burn until the jet is really hot, and then, timing your action carefully, you pump gently, like this ! "

He suited his actions to the words, and began pumping steadily. For a while nothing happened, and then there was a sudden rush of flame which leapt up with a roar and singed Hugh's eyebrows, causing him to jump back and bang his head against the boom which rested in the crutches across the top of the well.

"I see now," commented John, sarcastically, "you were quite right ; it only needs a little understanding ; quite simple ! "

"Brute ! " replied Hugh. "You don't deserve the cup of tea I was going to brew for you. By the time you've gone to get that precious radio of yours, I'll really have this thing going. I hope all the valves have busted on the way up ! " He rubbed the back of his head sorrowfully, and then set to work on the primus again. Soon it was roaring cheerfully, and the kettle began to sing. John came back with a smaller parcel, which he carried very gingerly, as if it was exceptionally fragile, and took it into the cabin, where he unpacked it quickly and gave it a swift examination.

"Seems to have survived the journey safely enough," he said ; "we'll try it out later on. I've persuaded the yacht-owner to let us have an extra accumulator, so that we shan't run out of electric light half-way."

"Good show. I've brewed some tea ; I

suggest we have a quick break now, and then push out into the river afterwards; we don't want to stay here tonight; too much like civilization."

With that, the two friends moved into the well, and ate a hurried and very impromptu meal, consisting largely of thick slabs of bread and honey, and large cupfuls of tea. After the first pangs of hunger had been satisfied, they took a longer look at the yacht which they had hired for their last holiday together before being called up for National Service.

" She looks handsome enough," remarked John. "You said you liked the look of her from the photograph in the catalogue, and I think you were right. None of that 'mast-stuck - right - forward - sluggish - as - a - barge' touch about her. Not like some of the tubs they hire on the Broads. I remember the first one I ever sailed in. It was described in the catalogue as 'Una-rigged; very easy to handle.' It certainly was. But oh! how dull! Even in a gale she wouldn't misbehave!"

" Yes, the fellow at the office seemed anxious to make quite sure that one of us had had some experience of sailing. He said that they had only recently converted this yacht into a full cabin cruiser; previously, she had been a day-boat, hired out only to approved customers who wanted to have her for use with their house-boats or bungalows. He said that the only snag is that she draws a little more water than most boats of her size, but she had to be keeled up rather more heavily because of her greater sail-area."

" Ah, well, I suppose we must make a move ; though I could easily turn in now. I must say those spring berths look very snug and tempting. I shan't be sorry to stretch my limbs on one tonight.   Those tandem saddles are not exactly armchairs ! "

With that they pushed the crockery into the metal-lined sink, and shut the lid down on it (this was called " patent washing-up "). Then they finished packing away their clothes in the drawers which pulled out from under the berths, pushed their cases into the roomy forepeak, cleared the well of loose odds and ends, and prepared to cast off.

" Senior and experienced member of the crew should take the quant pole ! " said Hugh. " Come along John, show your skill ! "

Grumbling softly, John pulled the long 12-foot pole, with its peculiarly-shaped end-piece, clear of the rigging, and prepared for action. Hugh had meanwhile jumped ashore, pulled up the stern rond anchor, and then taken his place at the tiller. John then went on to the bank, collected the bow anchor, gave the yacht a good strong heave by the shrouds, and leapt on board as she began to glide smoothly along the dyke towards the open river.   Then he went into action with the quant pole, giving gentle but steady pressure with the foot of the quant firmly in the bank so that it did not slip deeply into the mud. Hugh failed to check the sideways lunge sufficiently, so that John had to stop pushing and wait for the *Viking* to swing straight again. After some uncomplimentary remarks about steering a toy yacht, he soon had *Viking* out of the dyke and sliding steadily along with a slight tide running in their favour.

" Can't we moor up along here and set sail ? " queried Hugh. " D'you think it's worth it ? There's an hour to go before sunset. The breeze seems fairly steady."

" I don't quite know," replied John. " As we've started from Horning, we haven't that long tree-lined stretch from Wroxham to worry about, and there's usually quite good sailing from here downstream. Though there's that stretch by the water-works, where the trees blanket the wind . . . ." He paused, thoughtfully. " I don't think it's really worth the trouble," he went on. " We might have to quant again if the wind drops at sunset, and we can make a nice early start tomorrow. I'd like to get well on the way to Potter Heigham if I can by tomorrow evening. Come and take a turn at the quant. It's quite easy, just like lighting a primus ! "

" You didn't object to drinking the cup of tea, did you, smart one ! I'm game, anyhow."

With that they changed places, and Hugh bent himself to the task of quanting. It certainly had looked easy enough, and he slid the pole confidently into the water ; he felt it touch bottom and leaned hard upon it in the approved style. The pole continued to slide smoothly and speedily downwards, having struck a particularly soft patch in the river-bottom, and Hugh only just saved himself by a quick grab at the shrouds. Hardly had he prevented himself from falling face forwards into the water, when he realized that he had nearly lost the quant pole, the knob at the top of which was retreating steadily sternwards. He made a grab for it, holding on to the shrouds with one hand, and for a moment he hung precariously between the shrouds and the pole, nearly losing his grip on the varnished knob. Slowly and reluctantly the pole loosed itself from its slimy bed, whilst the yacht, slowed down by the sudden reverse pull, yawed considerably in the sluggish current, nearly losing steerage way. John worked hard with the rudder, and managed to keep her reasonably straight, but could not help remarking that he would love to have seen Hugh perched on the end of the pole in midstream. "Lots of perch about here," he remarked meaningfully. "Another queer fish in the river wouldn't make much difference ! Ha ! ha !"

Hardly had the laugh got under way, however, before it disappeared with startling speed. Hugh, heaving desperately at the quant pole, brought it rapidly and triumphantly to the surface. So rapidly, in fact, that he lost control and let the lower end, which was coated with thick black mud, fall back into the water beside the well.

" Ouch ! " cried John, as a liberal spattering of mud suddenly appeared on his face and over his shirt, " Clumsy great oaf ! What are you trying to do ? Kill a few fish for supper by the concussion process ? It's cleaner with gelignite, you know ! "

" So sorry, old man," murmured Hugh, in tones which belied his words. " Nice brand of mud they keep up here in Norfolk, isn't it ? You have developed measles suddenly ; shall we pull in for a doctor ? "

" Better to buy a book on yachtsmanship, I should think," muttered John. " Come on, get pushing again, for I've no control over her at all ; she's just drifting with the tide. Try again, and don't put your full weight on the pole until you strike something pretty firm." Then he began to sing, lugubriously, " Yo-o heave ho ! Yo-o hea-eave ho. . . ."

" Always did like that song," said Hugh. " Nothing quite like ' The Lily of Laguna ', in my opinion."

" That was ' The Volga Boat Song ', nitwit ; come on, do your stuff ! "

Some steady pushing by Hugh soon brought them round the bend in the river, and they tied up for the night in the lee of some bushes which formed a semi-circular opening giving access to the river bank, in which they firmly planted their anchors. Since they had not folded the awning right back when they left the boatyard, it was the work of a few minutes to put up the wooden supports ("technically known as 'spreaders,'" John informed his friend) and pull the thick canvas back over the well so that they were cosily shut in for the night. Hugh was busying himself with the belated washing-up, and with the preparations for supper, when he suddenly heard a call from John, who was on deck tidying up the ropes and making fast the awning.

"I say, Hugh, come and look at this!"

Hugh pushed his head out of the awning at the stern.

"What's to do?" he asked.

"Look at that yacht; what a beauty! I wonder where she's come from. Looks like a sea-going craft to me. See the Bermuda rig— that tall mast with the pointed mainsail running to the peak, without any gaff!"

The yacht in question, a smooth-lined, cleanly-built craft, varnished black with a thin gold line running from bow to stern just underneath the shallow gunwale, was sailing slowly downstream, heeling gently in the now failing breeze, her sails tinted golden in the rays of the setting sun.

"*Windward*, Wroxham," read Hugh, as he

scanned the yacht's stern. " I like her name."

" Yes," replied John, " she's certainly a fast-looking craft ; she should be mooring up soon. Perhaps we shall see her again : I should think she could leave us pretty cold if it came to a race ! "

There was a sudden pause in the conversation as both Hugh and John looked thoughtfully at the sluggishly-flowing water, scarcely rippled by the evening air. A deep hush seemed to have fallen over the whole scene as the sun set in a riot of red and gold. The reeds on the opposite bank whispered occasionally at the touch of the breeze, but the only sound which reached them was the occasional cry of a curlew, and the distant chime of a church clock ringing out the hour.

" There goes the *Windward*," said John, pointing to the tip of her mast which could be seen moving slowly above the line of bushes which bordered the river around the next bend. " We should be able to see her for another quarter-mile at least. She should be moored up by then. Come on, let's get on with supper—I'm feeling really hungry now. I vote we open one of those tins of sausage meat ! "

" Carried unanimously ! " replied Hugh. They both dived back under the awning, and busied themselves with primuses, tin-opener, vegetable-scraper, and all the paraphernalia of yachting cookery.

Soon all was ready ; they settled themselves in the cosy cabin, lit with a solitary 12-volt bulb, devoured an ample supper, read a while, yarned drowsily for a little longer, and then turned in, to sleep the sleep of those whose muscles are tired with healthy exercise, and whose minds are relaxed after long spells of concentration.

## Chapter 2

### HUGH LEARNS A THING OR TWO

HUGH was dreaming happily of flying a Meteor at incredible speeds (he was expecting to be called up into the Air Force) when he felt a heavy hand pummelling the small of his back, and a familiar voice bellowing in his ear : " Come on, you lazy landlubber ; show a leg there ! Eight bells and all's well ! "

" What have bells to do with it ? " he mumbled, " wasser time ? "

" Eight bells, you chump ; don't ask me what that is because I don't know ; all I know is that it's time to get up. I've looked through the porthole, and there's a ruffle on the water that speaks of a useful breeze. I'll clear up while you get the breakfast ready ; I wish we'd done that washing-up last night."

Hugh rolled out from the blankets, blinked sleepily for a moment or two, stretched his limbs, and then began to reach for his clothes. An old pair of flannels and a somewhat grimy sweater completed a first-rate yachtsman's outfit, and had the great advantage of being very easy to put on.

Breakfast was a somewhat hurried affair, for both John and Hugh (the latter especially, for this was his first holiday on the Broads) were keen to spread the sails in the steady breeze which was now blowing from the south-west.

"Let's get everything cleared away properly before we set sail," said John. "It's no joke trying to tack with half your cutlery sliding about the well. While you're finishing off, I'll connect my radio up, and try to get the Airmet weather broadcast ; we're some way from the transmitter at Dunstable, but as it's long-wave transmission I should just get it."

He disappeared into the cabin, reappearing a few moments later with an aerial wire which he attached to the pennant ; then he ran it expertly up the mast, and set to work on the pride of his heart—his high-power all-wave radio set. He had adapted it from a war-surplus Service set, and could use it also as a low-power transmitter. Soon a faint voice, with a North-country accent, could be heard giving " details of the weather situation at o-seven hundred hours." The " situation " looked good. Steady south-westerly to southerly breezes of moderate strength were expected in the eastern half of England for at least twenty-four hours.

John could never resist the temptation to do a little knob-twiddling once he had his set working, and so, under the pretext of " testing out conditions around here," he idly ran round the short-wave bands before switching off. A rapid succession of voices, in several languages, of music in several contrasting styles, and of high-pitched morse signals followed one another as he turned the slow-motion dials. Suddenly he stopped.

" I say, Hugh," he said, " listen to this ! "

All that Hugh could hear was a loud succession of morse signals against a background of strong humming. " What's special about that ? " he asked.

" Whoever that chap is," said John, " he's very near—almost on top of us, I should think."

" Probably a cargo vessel just off the coast—it's only a dozen miles or so away from here," suggested Hugh.

" Sounds nearer than that, almost next door to us. . . . Some sort of code he's using," said John, after listening for a few minutes. " I wonder who it can be. I don't remember seeing an amateur station registered just near here in the official list. Must be a ship, after all."

" In any case, we can't stop to investigate now," urged Hugh. " I've finished clearing up, and I want to see what those sails look like unfurled."

" All right," said John, regretfully switching off his precious set, " you take the starboard side —that's the right, you know—and I'll take the port ; we'll get the awning tidily folded and stowed."

" Thanks for the information ! It was kind of you to remember my inexperience so tactfully,"

replied Hugh, sarcastically. " Did you tie these
so-called knots when you lashed the awning
down last night ? It must have been dark.
Time you joined the Wolf Cubs, my friend ! "

" No insubordination, or you'll have to walk
the plank—if we can find a plank ! "

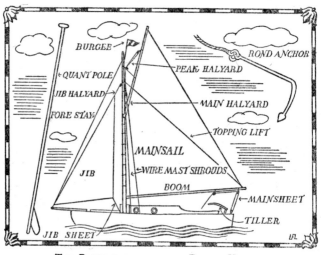

THE RIGGING OF A TYPICAL BROADS YACHT

Soon the awning and sail-cover were safely
stowed below, in the forepeak, and John was
checking over the ropes (" technically known as
' halyards,' " he observed, condescendingly)
before hoisting sail.

" Jump ashore and get the stern rond anchor,"
said John, as he began to heave on the peak and
throat halyards, causing the gaff to rise slowly,
horizontally, with the white canvas unfolding

and flapping in the breeze beneath it. Soon the mainsail was hoisted to John's expert satisfaction (he had sailed a good deal, including four or five trips on the Broads), and the *Viking* was swaying with her stern out towards midstream, gently swinging as the wind and the tide took her in charge by turns.

Meanwhile John had shackled on the jib-sheets (" *You* know them as ' ropes,' " he added thoughtfully, but without receiving any appreciation) and was hauling on the halyard until the large loose-footed sail was flapping vigorously.

" I'll soon put a stop to that flapping about," said Hugh, as he pulled on the rope which led back from the jib to the well, where he had taken his stand at the tiller.

John said nothing.

Suddenly *Viking* lurched violently, straining at the bow anchor. Then she heeled over and lurched with equal violence in the opposite direction. Hugh sat down with a rather heavy bump. " What did that ? " he enquired, bracing himself for the next shock. "Has the wind got up suddenly, or something ? "

" If you'll kindly slacken off that jib-sheet which you made fast just now, we might get a little peace," suggested John. " I thought you might as well learn from experience, while the breeze is not too strong, that there are times when it's safest to let a sail have its own way. You can turn a boat like this over as easy as winking by simply holding the sail in at the wrong moment ! "

Hugh quickly loosened the rope which he had so carefully fastened to the cleat on the side of the well, and *Viking* steadied herself as the sail, now flapping noisily, was freed of restraint, and no longer served as a lever by which the wind could act on the yacht.

After a final inspection, to see that all the ropes were running free, John pulled on the front mooring-rope, jumped ashore from the bows, pulled up the anchor which had been well and truly sunk in the bank, and leapt back on to the foredeck.    Listening carefully for the rustle of a gust of wind across the reeds on the marshes, he suddenly called out to Hugh, who was at the tiller, " Hard over with the tiller—to your right, nitwit ! "

Then he skipped back into the well, hauled in hard on the starboard jib-sheet, and waited while the wind filled the sail and swung the bows off from the bank.    Meanwhile the mainsail, running free, was swinging farther and farther out to port (" that's the left-hand side, young man," remarked John, ducking to avoid the inevitable retort).    When *Viking* was well out into the stream, he pulled in the mainsail, which immediately stiffened as it filled with wind and began to thrust the yacht smoothly forward.

" She's sailing ! " cried Hugh, exultantly.    It

was the first time he had felt the smooth, vibrant, driving force of moving air, and it was a sweet and satisfying sensation. As *Viking* cleared the line of small trees which had sheltered her during the night, she felt the full force of what was by now a stiff south-westerly breeze, and began to heel gracefully to one side as she picked up speed. Soon they were cutting along at a fair pace, and Hugh's delight was plain to see as he watched the sails, now taut and full of wind. John had trimmed them satisfactorily, and was bearing up on the tiller to counteract the tug of the wind, which seemed determined to pull *Viking's* bows round to starboard.

The broad river here began to turn in a north-easterly direction, and, as they rounded the bend, John gave the mainsail plenty of sheet, so that the boom jutted out to port, almost at right-angles to the direction in which they were sailing. The mast quivered a little under the heavy thrust of the large sail, but, as John pointed out, the wire shrouds were now proving their worth by taking the greater part of the strain.

" Yes," said Hugh, " it rather worried me at first when I saw how slack they were ; I nearly suggested that we should tighten them up before we started, but I realize now that some allowance is made for the natural springiness of the mast."

" Quite correct, O observant one," said John, " you'll be able to take your exam for

First Cabin Boy's ticket if you go on at that rate."

"Can't I take over for a little while now?" asked Hugh. "The wind is right behind us, so there's nothing to go wrong for the next half-mile or so."

John pondered a moment. "All right," he said. "Keep her in the middle of the stream, and keep the mainsail full of wind."

He handed the tiller and the loose end of the mainsheet to his friend, who thereupon adopted a post which he vainly hoped looked like a mixture of Lord Nelson and Sir Thomas Lipton, and took over control. John did not move very far away, however, and seemed more concerned with what was happening to the rear edge of the mainsail than with anything else. At first Hugh kept his eyes steadily fixed on the river ahead, but as he gained confidence he began to survey the passing scene. Once or twice he had to change direction rather suddenly as *Viking* quickly went off her course if he did not check the tiller constantly.

John said nothing, but moved a little nearer the tiller, and kept his eye on the sail and on the blue and red pennant which flew at the masthead.

"There's nothing in this sailing business, after all," observed Hugh. "To think that I imagined yachting to be difficult!" (This with an air of complete mastery.) "Look at that fellow pike-fishing from his punt," he went on.

John continued looking at the leach of the mainsail, which was now flapping vigorously, although the wind was aft. *Viking* swung round to port a little as Hugh tried to see where the pike-fisher's float was.

Then it happened. Hugh suddenly noticed that all the strain had gone from the mainsheet, which was now slack in his hand. As he noticed this, John pushed him on one side and made a grab for the mainsheet and the tiller.

" What's the grand idea . . . ? " began Hugh, standing up to his full height with an air of injured innocence. He said no more, however, for he suddenly realized that the mainsail was swinging over to the other side, and the boom was coming straight for his head. He ducked as quickly as he could, but was a little too late, and it grazed the top of his head sharply as it passed over. *Viking* lurched with the sudden change of balance, but John, who had been waiting for precisely this to happen, eased the shock by steering up-wind for a moment, and paying out the last of the mainsheet as smoothly as he could. When the mainsail filled with wind on the other quarter *Viking* lurched again, throwing Hugh on to the floor, where he sat rubbing the top of his head ruefully.

" That," said John, as he got the yacht under control again, " was a gybe."

" Jolly poor sort of joke, I reckon," was Hugh's somewhat rattled reply.

"I mean g-y-b-e, not j-i-b-e, brainless! Don't you remember reading about that in your little book of words? I thought the best way for you to get the idea would be by experience, so I let you take over, and I kept at hand ready for trouble. The fact is that you are never in more danger in a yacht than when you are sailing along with a strong breeze dead behind; unless you keep your mainsail full of wind, and the head of the boat a little up-wind, you're likely to have that happen. The idea is to keep things under control, so that *you* decide when she gybes; then you can control it easily enough."

"I see," replied Hugh. "Well, that's one way of knocking the corners off a novice!"

"Have you seen any sign of the *Windward*?" asked John some time later, as they reached the end of a straight stretch. "She can't have come much farther than this, unless she sailed after dark—and that's not usual in these waters, especially as there was no moon."

"Certainly seems to have disappeared," said Hugh. "I don't remember seeing any mooring or channel where she could have tied up without our seeing her. Perhaps she sailed before we did this morning. We seem to have beaten everybody else, though; it's still quite early."

"She must have got away before us. I wonder where she's bound for?"

"Maybe we shall see her again; meanwhile, I vote we have a little coffee with which to drown my sorrows ; keep her as steady as you can, and I'll really show you how to light a primus."

Hugh delved into a couple of lockers, and soon had the primus roaring cheerfully in its zinc-lined compartment ; by the time the kettle had boiled, *Viking* had rounded the next bend, had passed the stretch of water from which the Yarmouth Water Works had their intake, where mooring was forbidden, and was beating down a stretch of the river which ran almost due south.

" I was going to suggest that we moored up to drink our elevenses," said Hugh, as he finished off the delicate task of brewing the coffee ; " but I think I'd rather keep sailing while this breeze holds. Let's have a look at the map."

He unfolded the large-scale map which they carried, and they quickly found their position.

" Why not sail into Ranworth Broad, and have a quick look round there ?  We've plenty of time if the breeze holds."

" It's a bit awkward getting in and out," said John.  " There are rather a lot of trees about, but with this wind I should think we could sail most of the way.  Right you are, then ; hand me up my coffee, and hold tight as we turn into the entrance channel."

This latter was a short, narrow stretch of water, at the end of which was an even narrower entrance to the Broad itself.  A thick cluster of trees meant that the wind came uncertainly into their sails.  Once or twice they found themselves

losing way altogether as they turned on to a new
tack ; then, when they had lost all rudder control,
owing to the yacht being stationary in the water, a
gust of wind would catch the sails and send them
drifting sideways, right off their course. However,
with the help of some hefty shoves on the quant
pole, they reached the open water, and sailed
cheerfully round the beautiful, tree-lined lake.
A half-sunken, derelict house-boat lay on the
mud near the entrance. A small motor boat
was tied up at the village staithe in the far corner ;
and a couple of yachts had apparently been dismasted and laid up for the winter close by.
They had the whole stretch of water to themselves, and enjoyed not only the sway and surge
of the sailing itself, but the very lovely setting
of the Broad. They completed one circuit, and
then made their way out through the narrow
entrance again, and into the main stream.

Just after they had left Ranworth, they pulled
into the bank, and moored up for a few moments
while John checked over one of the jib halyards
which had come loose on its cleat, with the result
that the sail was flapping in a most unseamanlike
manner. After he had tightened it and re-
fastened it securely, they sat for a few moments
resting, and enjoying the wild beauty of the reed-
lined, sluggish river.

Overhead, puffy white cumulous clouds were
moving fairly rapidly across the sky (" but not
getting any bigger—which is a good sign,"

remarked Hugh, who prided himself on his weather lore). The considerable patches of clear
sky gave a blue tone to the water, and every-
where was calm and quiet. Away to the south
they could see the spire of Ranworth church,
which stood out on what was for those parts a
prominent hill. Its bells were ringing out the
call to worship, and their music carried clearly
across to the river.

" Sounds lovely, doesn't it ? " commented
Hugh. " It seems more natural to think about
going to church when you're out in the wilds like
this. In town we can hardly hear the bells for
the din of the traffic. Still, I suppose we must
write the whole religious business off as a beautiful relic of the good old days ; there doesn't seem
to be much room for that sort of thing in this
scientific and streamlined world."

" I don't know," replied John, " I've had a
bit of a shock this summer. At the place where
the family went for a holiday, there were some
young fellows holding meetings for children on
the beach—they called themselves the ' Sizzem,'
or ' C.S.S.M. ' ; Children's Seaside Services
Mission, I think it was. They seemed rather
intelligent chaps, and I got talking to one of
them one evening after a meeting. He was a
university type, who had seen some pretty
strenuous service during the war, and he talked
about Christ as if he knew Him personally.
It was real enough to him—the sort of clear-cut

faith that those chaps must have had when they first came to convert the heathen in these parts ! "

" H'm. I don't know. Probably psychological," was Hugh's reply. " I say, what's this coming round the bend ? The *Windward*, I'll be bound ! ! Where's she sprung from ? It looks as if we must have passed her this morning, but I could swear she was not in sight ; perhaps she's got a private hide-out, or something ! "

Four keen young eyes scanned her carefully as she bowled along in the now spanking breeze, sailing close to the wind, but making a fair number of knots as she heeled over gracefully.

" Did you notice anything queer about her ? " asked John, as she began to turn the next bend.

" Can't say that I did," replied Hugh, " though I'd love to know where she tied up last night."

" There was rather a lot of gear at the top of her mast," said John, thinking aloud, " and more halyards than usual with a Bermuda rig ; I don't know what she would want all that for."

" I shouldn't let it worry you ; these Broads yachts often have gadgets which their owners have designed, or taken a fancy to. Let's get moving again ; we ought to get to St. Benet's Abbey for lunch ; I've just checked up on the map again, and it's only about one mile as the roach swims."

" Right-ho," said John, easing off the topping-lift so that the mainsail smoothed itself out to its proper shape. " You go forward and set up the

jib again ; then you can stand by to get the
anchor ; I'll take her off from the shore whilst
standing at the tiller ; it will be useful practice."

Hugh went forward, and began to heave on
the jib halyard (after trying one or two of the
other halyards with somewhat unexpected results !). Carefully watching the rope to see
that it did not foul any of the others, he failed
to notice that as the jib-sail filled with wind, it
became violently active—with the result that he
received several hearty slaps in the face from the
fiercely flapping canvas. John laughed un-
sympathetically, but soon Hugh had mastered
the tricks which the seemingly demon-inspired
sail was trying to play on him, and had set it
up well and truly. Then he pulled on the rope
which led to the anchor, embedded in the shore,
and when *Viking* was near enough, jumped on
to the bank. He gripped the anchor, and when
he had drawn it from the soft earth he took a
flying jump back on to the foredeck.

" Keep clear of the jib," shouted John, from
the well. " Stand by the mast, hold tight, and
look out for trouble ! "

Then John pulled the starboard jib-sheet, so
that the bows of *Viking* were drawn away from
the bank, released it slightly, hauled gently on
the mainsail, and as it began to draw the yacht
moved forwards downstream once again. Hugh
walked carefully back along the narrow deck
into the well, keeping a watchful eye upon the

boom which could have swept him off the boat altogether if it had come across at the wrong moment.

It was straightforward and speedy sailing now, past the dyke which led down to Horning Hall and on to the broad stretch of water where the River Ant joined the main stream.

" What's that tower thing over there ? " asked Hugh, as they rounded a bend in the river. " Looks like a huge windmill gone to ruin ! "

" That's what it is," said John. " But it's more than that really ; if you look when we get closer, you'll see that it is built into the ruins of an old Abbey ; that is actually St. Benet's Abbey. There isn't much left, I'm afraid ; the folk around here used the stones to build their own barns and farmhouses, but the foundations have been traced out, and there's no doubt it must have been a massive building when it was in its glory. We'll have lunch here, and maybe we'll have time to explore it afterwards."

## Chapter 3

### JOHN AND HUGH RECEIVE A VISITOR

JOHN and Hugh had finished lunch, and were having a short rest before setting sail, when John, who had switched on his radio again, having hastily rigged up his aerial, aroused his drowsy companion.

"Hugh! There it is again! Same wavelength and modulation. And it really is near us. It's the same transmitter as yesterday."

Sure enough, the same powerful morse signals were coming out of the speaker. Hugh, who had been very keen on morse whilst in the A.T.C., began transcribing them, writing in pencil on an envelope which was lying at the foot of his bed.

"But that certainly doesn't make sense," he said. "They must be using one of the commercial codes. Listen to that! Just a string of numbers. Now they're repeating something; hear it? Three times—now they've stopped transmitting; that must have been their signing-off signal. Two dots and two dashes."

John spun the dials quickly, listening closely, with the volume full on. A hideous succession of noises came from the speaker, and then John stopped. "Listen!"

Sure enough, there was the same signal,

though very faint indeed. It was once repeated ("Must have missed one," remarked Hugh) and then followed by a further series of morse signals. Hugh took a few more of the numbers down, but soon wearied of a rather pointless occupation, and gave the paper to John, who glanced blankly at what was written.

"It would be interesting to put a directional aerial on to that reply," he said. "We might get some idea of where it came from. Probably from Marconi's or one of the Post Office stations. Ah, well ; we must stir ourselves to action, or we shall never reach Potter Heigham."

He went out into the well to prepare for moving off, and began putting the dishes away into the lockers, when he felt vaguely uncomfortable, as if he were not alone. He looked up, and there on the bank, surveying him with a searching, questioning look, was a stranger whom he recognized as the man who had been at the tiller of the *Windward* that morning. And farther along the river bank, some forty yards away, was *Windward* herself, moored to an old post which was all that was left of the former well-timbered dyke supports.

"Good afternoon," said the stranger pleasantly. "You're taking a holiday late this year ?"

He obviously expected some sort of reply, but John somehow felt he ought to be on his guard, and gave a very abrupt and non-committal answer. The stranger was a middle-aged man, powerfully built, and obviously very fit, with an erect, somewhat military bearing. (" Retired colonel, or something," thought John. " Jolly nice life, careering around in a lovely yacht like that ! ")

" That's a powerful radio you have there," persisted the man from the *Windward.* " I couldn't help hearing it as I strolled past your yacht. Must stretch one's legs sometimes— that's the snag with these small craft."

" Yes," replied John, " it's a hobby of mine."

" Reception's very good round here," went on the stranger, seemingly determined to make conversation in spite of John's calculated stand-offishness. " They say you can get the Continental stations particularly well in these parts. We've got a little set on board, but I haven't taken much interest in it."

" I have heard that also.    I haven't really had time to try things out."

" Will you be staying long ? "

" We've booked for a fortnight."

" Do you know the Broads very well ? "

" Just a little.    Excuse me a moment, I believe my friend wants me. Good-bye.  May see you again.    I'd like to race *Viking* against *Windward* sometime ! "    With that somewhat feeble excuse John dived into the cabin, leaving the stranger to walk slowly back to his yacht.   John eyed him carefully through a slight crack left by the partly-closed cabin doors.

" Jolly inquisitive customer, Hugh.   I think

he would have gone on to ask our life-history if
I hadn't been rather rude. What's it to do
with him whether we have a radio or not ?
It's not an offence to listen in. I don't like that
chap. Seemed too pleasant to be true. I'd like
to have a race with his sleek little *Windward*, and
really beat him up. But I doubt whether we
could hold him. Certainly not until we've had a
bit more experience with *Viking*."

"Hullo ! " said Hugh. "She's setting sail ;
those chaps know their stuff."

The stranger who had spoken to John had been
joined by another, possibly the only other,
member of the crew, a fair-haired, rather lean-
looking younger man, aged about twenty-five
Between them, the two men had hoisted the sails
and set their yacht in motion in a matter of a
few moments.

"I suppose he had been up the Ant to Ludham
Bridge, after he passed us," remarked John,
"otherwise he wouldn't have been behind us
again. Not unless he's just wasting time, and had
come back again to St. Benet's Abbey."

"Seems in a hurry now," said Hugh, nodding
in the direction of the rapidly disappearing
*Windward*. She was a beautiful sight as she
heeled hard over in the now fresh wind. Soon
only her masthead was visible as she rounded
one of the innumerable curves in the river and
made towards Thurne Mouth.

"Let's follow along and see which way she

goes," said John. " Now's your chance to get
the sails set quickly."

The two friends went hurriedly to work and
soon *Viking* was following *Windward* downstream,
with the wind blowing hard most of the while on
the starboard beam. There was really enough
strength in the breeze to justify their taking a
reef in the mainsail, but with the excitement of a
chase in their blood they were not inclined to
stop for anything like that.

" Hold hard," said John, as his ears caught the
sound of a squall whistling through the reeds
on its way towards the boat. The *Viking*,
already heeling over quite sharply, yielded to
the further pressure, and dipped the edge of the
deck beneath the water as John held her reso-
lutely on her course. He eased the mainsheet
out a little to prevent her going too far over and
losing speed through lying on her beam, but kept
her sailing hard, so that Hugh, who was having
the thrill of his life, was busily engaged in rescuing
straying equipment as it slid about the cabin.
Ominous noises came from the crockery lockers,
and the saucepans added their contribution to
the general din, but the two yachtsmen were
not sparing much thought for such details ;
the reckoning could come later. They were
*sailing*, really *sailing*, and as the wind whistled
through the ropes, and sighed across the marshes,
they felt the inward surge of pride and defiance
which only those men know who pit themselves

against the elements. Theirs was the special thrill of knowing that they were not only defying this seemingly irresistible force which swept unseen across the unhindering levels, they were harnessing it, compelling it to drive them along, mastering it as a skilled rider masters a rebellious, unbroken colt. This was *life*!

"Where's the *Windward*, John?" asked Hugh, suddenly.

"About a mile ahead, I should say," was the reply. "I think we're gaining on her a little, but she's obviously not going all out—they don't seem in any particular hurry; it would speed them up somewhat if we began to overtake them, I guess. We shall soon see which way they are going, for Thurne Mouth is only another mile or so ahead. Come on, *Viking*, stick it, old lady! You're doing fine."

John ran his eye over the sails with a satisfied look. Mainsail and jib were taut and trim, each adding its full quota of drive, causing the tall mast to quiver as the yacht drove swiftly forward, surging with extra speed as a gust periodically caught up with her. Her wash ran along the bank behind, doubling back on itself, and leaving little isolated whirlpools in the holes which the passage of many boats had worn in the dykes. Hugh took the tiller for a while, and, despite one or two somewhat wild lunges, kept *Viking* steady on her course down the middle of the stream.

" John, do you know where that little telescope of yours is ?  I'd like to borrow it," suddenly asked Hugh, who had been looking keenly at she mast of the *Windward* for a few moments.

" Right-ho," said John.  He dived into the cabin, and emerged shortly afterwards with a pocket telescope, which he drew out to its correct length, and then handed to Hugh, taking the tiller and mainsheet from him in return.

Hugh fixed the telescope on the yacht ahead, looked carefully for a moment, and then said, excitedly,

" They're hauling something up the mast, John.  You said something about some extra halyards.  See if you can see what it is."

John took the powerful little glass, and looked for a minute or so, then dashed into the cabin, saying,

" It's an aerial ; a rather special one, too, by the look of it.  I can't see the details, but it's obviously out-of-the-ordinary.  I'm going to turn on the set and see if we can hear anything.  He might be the mystery transmitter."

" Couldn't be that, because he was next to us at St. Benet's Abbey, and he didn't have his aerial up then although we heard the signals."

" Yes, I hadn't thought of that," pondered John.  " But there it is, nevertheless ! "

Out of the loudspeaker came the same powerful morse signals.  Two dots, two dashes, repeated twice, then a further series of code numbers.

"It must be just a coincidence," said Hugh. "He's probably got a powerful receiver on board, that's all."

"But supposing there are two transmitters, one on the boat there, and one in a house or bungalow nearby," suggested John. "They might both use the same call-sign, and be working together."

"That's an idea ; see what he signs off with."

Suddenly there was a pause, and then the signal, two dots, two dashes, repeated twice.

"That's very queer," said John. "You don't usually find people taking transmitters with them on yacht trips on the Broads. Still, if he is a sea-going craft, it's understandable."

"There he goes, straight up the Thurne towards Potter Heigham. Looks as if we shall meet again," said Hugh.

## Chapter 4

### THE VINCENT FAMILY IS INTRODUCED

THE *Viking* moored up to the bank near the two bridges at Potter Heigham just before six o'clock that evening, after careering furiously along with a strong wind almost dead aft.

" How are we going to stop ? " asked Hugh, as they came into the last half-mile straight before the bridge.  " We obviously can't sail under that poky little affair, and I don't see for the life of me how we can stop this outfit, now ! "

" Oh, you just jump ashore with the anchor, and hold tight ; if that doesn't work, you put the brakes on," suggested John, helpfully.

" No, Sir ; not this child ! " was Hugh's reply. " Just as soon try and stop a bulldozer with a matchbox ! "

" Then you'll simply have to wait and see," retorted John.

As they came up nearer the bridge, they saw that *Windward* was moored at a private stretch of the bank which belonged to one of the boat-yards.  (" Well known round here," commented Hugh.)

On the right-hand bank, which was public mooring, there was one other yacht, which was obviously in commission, together with several dismasted hulls of boats which were presumably being laid up for the winter.

John began to haul the mainsail in when they were some way from the bridge, thus "spoiling" it to some extent, for the wind was still aft. As the *Viking* slowed, he picked out his spot, a fairly long vacant stretch of the right bank, sailed a little way past it, ordered Hugh forward ready to jump ashore with the bow rond anchor, and then with a sudden " Hold tight ! " he let slip both the sails, dropped the peak, put the rudder hard over, and swung the *Viking* round in a semicircle. It was then a simple matter to edge her into the bank, so that by the time she had reached the mooring-place, which he had deliberately overshot on the run up, she was nearly stationary. Hugh stepped easily ashore, and made her fast by the bows and stern.

" Now you know how to stop a yacht," added John, with just a tinge of pride in his voice.

The yacht which was moored next to *Viking* was apparently, like themselves, on a holiday cruise. It was also a slim, fast-looking craft and had a general appearance of being well managed ; the decks were clean and the whole appearance trim and tidy. From the sound of voices which could occasionally be heard faintly across the gap between them, John and Hugh gathered that there were at least two men and one girl on board ; and they amused themselves, as they ate their tea, trying to imagine what the strangers would really look like when they came on deck.

" The girl seems quite young, judging by her voice," thought Hugh.

" So is one of the men," suggested John.

They were both right.

A few minutes later the crew of the other yacht stepped on to the bank one after the other. There was a girl, aged about sixteen, neatly but not showily dressed ; a young man, obviously her brother, about a year or so older ; and a much older man, with slightly grey hair, whom they addressed variously as " Daddy," or " Pop," or " Father."

" I say, I know that fellow," said John, as the newcomers stood talking for a moment, and checking up to see that their boat was safely moored. " That's Dick Vincent ; I met him at the Cadet Camp in July—he's a very nice chap, somewhat quieter than most, and with rather queer ideas on religion, but straight as a die, and very friendly. Fancy meeting him up here ! "

Just then the family group came along the bank, passing the *Viking* on their way to the nearby road. John gave a smile of recognition as they passed by, and immediately the other fellow recognized him.

" John Wilson ! Hullo ! My, this is a surprise ! Jolly glad to see you. This is my sister, Christine, and this is Father. Dad and Chris, this is John Wilson, who was with me at Cadet

Camp in July ; you remember the fellow I told you about, who couldn't miss the bull's-eye on the Rifle Range if he tried."

" Jolly glad to meet you again," said John, hurriedly clearing his mouth, and introducing Hugh. " This is my friend Hugh Rogerson."

" We're celebrating Father's homecoming after eight years abroad," explained Dick Vincent, smilingly. " We're sailing *Sabrina* 2 ; not such a dashing name as your craft has ; I like the name *Viking*. We'll have to see which really is the faster ! You'll excuse us now, won't you ; we're off to the village Chapel, and the Service starts at six-thirty. See you again soon. Cheerio ! "

" Cheerio ! " echoed John and Hugh.

" You did say something about religion, didn't you, John ? "

" Yes ; those were Bibles which they were carrying ; did you notice ? "

" Yes, I noticed all right ; but there doesn't seem to be anything stuffy about that family. I wonder where Mrs. Vincent is."

" I seem to remember Dick saying something about her having been killed in an air-raid out in China. Mr. Vincent is a doctor, if I remember rightly."

" Hm. At any rate, they should provide some interesting company ; I should think that our two yachts would have a pretty even race if we get an opportunity ! . . . I say ! Don't turn round, but someone's having a good look at us through one of the portholes of the jolly old *Windward* ; she's nearly opposite us, and I can see the face of that fair-headed chap partly hidden by the little curtain. They must be very inquisitive travellers ; or perhaps they're admiring the way we keep the *Viking* ship-shape."

" I doubt it ; come on, let's get the washing-up finished, and then we can go for a stroll before we turn in.  It will soon be dark, and we could do with some exercise."

So saying, John set to work clearing the decks and unfurling the awning, while Hugh washed up and cleaned the well.  Soon the sails were stowed and the awning drawn protectingly over. The two friends jumped ashore, and set out for a stroll in the twilight.

They turned left, walked over the river bridge, pausing to watch the speed of the current as the tide, now ebbing, rushed through the narrow tunnel made by the low-built archway.

" It can be tricky work getting through there when the tide is running," remarked John. " Best time is either at low or high tide, when the water is slack.  The only snag is that some craft can't get through at high tide as their deck hamper is too high above the water level ; I think we should do it either way."

They resumed their walk, and were just passing a cottage, a little way along the road, when they heard the familiar voice of a B.B.C.

announcer coming through an open doorway :

> "This is the B.B.C. Light Programme.
> Here is the seven o'clock news.  The Prime
> Minister has spoken at a great rally in Bir-
> mingham this afternoon, saying that unless
> coal production is still further increased, to
> a level at least as great as pre-war, there will
> have to be further severe cuts in imports
> of foodstuffs. . . .   The drive against politi-
> cal agitators working on behalf of foreign
> powers is to be intensified.  It is thought that
> a number of dangerous members of an alien
> organization may be at large at the present
> time. . . . In an aeroplane disaster in France,
> fifteen people lost their lives when a Bellatrix
> air liner crashed at Le Bourget. . . . Britain's
> new experimental supersonic aircraft had
> its first flight-trials off the Western Ap-
> proaches today.  No details have been re-
> leased."

Hugh and John walked on.

"Nothing very startling," commented John.
"The headlines tell you all you want to know."

"Yes ; who are these political agitators they
keep talking about ? "

"They come from Diamatia ; it's the old game
—stirring up trouble in our industries, weakening
our recovery drive.  It gives the Diamatians a
better chance of getting a grip on their mid-
European neighbours."

"They're welcome !  I say, it's a good job
these cottages are strung out along the road like

this—they just about give enough light from their windows to keep us out of the ditch. It's pretty dangerous, I should think, when it gets really dark."

They continued their walk as far as the level crossing, watched a somewhat dilapidated train go through (" The second one this week," commented John), and then retraced their steps in the direction of the river. Darkness had by now settled heavily upon the lonely road, and they had to watch carefully as they strolled slowly along.

## Chapter 5

### TROUBLE BEGINS

G RADUALLY, John and Hugh became aware
of the voices of another group of people
walking in the same direction, some way in front of
them, and as they increased their pace they began
to catch up with this group. Then they saw, in
the light from a cottage window, that it was the
Vincent family. Mr. Vincent was in the middle,
with Dick on his right and Christine on his left ;
arms linked, talking merrily, they were also
stepping out briskly.

As Hugh and John came alongside, Dick
noticed them, and greeted them cheerily :
" What a grand evening ! I think this is the
best time of the year to have a holiday. Better
than stewing in cadet uniform in a heat-wave in
July, eh, John ? "

The friends had intended to walk on ahead,
but this direct approach led them straightway
into conversation, and they walked five abreast
down the lane riverwards.

" I'll say ! " replied John. " And I'd rather
be my own master on a yacht than be drilled
around in army boots on hard roads ! "

" If you had taken my advice, and joined the
A.T.C., you'd have saved yourself a lot of
trouble," suggested Hugh, mischievously.

" If you hadn't chosen your occasion so carefully, my young friend (John was two months older) you would be scragged by now," was John's vigorous reply. " Little boys playing with model aeroplanes ! What a show ! "

" Just as good as your wooden rifles, any old day ! "

At this point Mr. Vincent intervened.

" I think I am neutral in this discussion," he said. " So before there's any shedding of blood over it, I suggest we drop the subject, and try again."

" Carried unanimously," said Christine, in a voice which Hugh thought rather pleasant. " How long are you going to be up here ? "

John replied, " A fortnight ; we only started yesterday. What about yourselves ? "

" The same ; but we got away to an early start, and reached here by last night ; we've been moored up all day. We went to the village Church this morning and we've tried the Chapel this evening. It was jolly good, too, wasn't it, Dick ? "

" Well, I should hardly have called it a cultured sermon this evening. The minister was what they call a ' local preacher ', " he explained. " But I must say the man seemed to mean every word he said, and I've heard far less interesting sermons from far better educated preachers. What do you say, Dad ? "

There was something of respect and understanding conveyed in the very tone of Dick's voice when he spoke to his father ; John particularly was impressed by the whole relationship, so free and yet so respectful, which appeared to exist between them.

"I quite agree," said the doctor. "I felt that that preacher tonight was very much like some of the Chinese preachers whom I have heard. (I have just come back from China, you see.) He wouldn't do very well at some of the examinations which ministers have to pass in this country ; but I guess he'll pass with honours in the only exam. which really matters."

Hugh wanted to ask him what he meant by that phrase, but Dick interrupted him, saying, " We mustn't weary you with what we've been doing ; how have you been getting on today ? "

John told them how they had sailed through from Horning, and how they had been puzzled by the disappearance of the *Windward*.

"Oh, yes," said Dick ; " she came in just before you ; looks a very smart outfit. I only saw one member of her crew on deck ; the fair-headed one whom you mention did not put in an appearance."

By now they were back at the river, and making their way in single file along the bank to their respective moorings. A light shone through one of the portholes on the *Windward*, but most of them were shaded with interior curtains. Very soon other lights began to sparkle

on the coldly-flowing water as *Viking* and *Sabrina*
turned on their cabin lights. Hugh busied himself brewing cocoa, while John rigged his aerial,
and prepared to indulge in a few minutes' knob-
twiddling at his radio set. After some minutes'
silence, Hugh pushed his face inside the cabin.

" What's up ? Won't she go ? " he asked.

" No," said John, looking puzzled. " Seems
quite dead. It was all right at teatime. Perhaps it's because we've got the light on. It
shouldn't make any difference, but I'll try the
other accumulator." He changed the terminals
over, but to no effect. Then he disconnected
and unscrewed the back cover of the set, looking
expertly at the various connections. Finally, he
connected up again, switched on, and continued
his scrutiny.

" I think the valves must be dead," he said
suddenly, in a tone of dismay. He tried them
one by one, and then turned to Hugh saying,
" That's queer ; one valve is completely useless ;
and that happens to be the most important one
of the lot. I could probably rewire it to work
without one of the others, but I must have that
one going. I can't understand it at all. It's had
no shock."

John took the suspected valve out of its socket,
and tested it again with his pocket test-meter.
" It's dead all right ! " he said ; in such sorrowful
tones that Hugh could not resist remarking,
" And you sound as if you're reading the funeral

service ; cheer up, John ! it's only a valve after all ! "

" Only a valve, indeed !   But that's messed my set up for the holiday.   What beats me is why it should have gone ; these valves were specially built to withstand war service conditions, and they shouldn't simply fade out like that.   I could understand it if some ass had mixed the terminals up and put the high tension through the filament ; but you haven't been near the set ! "

" Say that again, and you won't have any set left at all ! " was Hugh's reply to John's sally.

" I say, look ! ! " Hugh went on.   " What's this on the floor ?   Somebody's visiting card, or what is it ? "

He bent down and pulled from a corner, where it had been partly hidden beneath an overhanging blanket, a small, folded, white card. " That wasn't there when we went out this evening ; I swept the floor right over.   It doesn't belong to you, does it ? "   John looked at it for a moment or two.

" No," he said, emphatically, " I've never seen it before.   What's it say ? "

Hugh opened it up.   " That's queer ; it looks like a list of dates to me."   He showed it to John. They both read :

$$1\text{-}10/10 \quad - \quad D.T. \; 15/9$$
$$11\text{-}20/10 \quad - \quad D.T. \; 25/9$$
$$21\text{-}30/10 \quad - \quad D.T. \; 5/10$$

and other figures similarly arranged. Altogether there were ten rows of numbers. There was nothing on the outside, and no other printing on the card.

"Whatever those figures mean," said John, "someone has been in here this evening! I wonder. . . . Yes! I've got it; that's why my radio won't work. Somebody's deliberately messed it up!"

He looked at the set more closely. "I think it has been interfered with," he went on. "I don't remember seeing those scratches by the screws on the back panel before. It looks as if someone tried to undo them with an ordinary type of screwdriver, and didn't come prepared to deal with a square-headed screw of this type. I wonder who it could have been; and why should anyone want to put this set out of commission, anyhow?"

"Everything else seems to be in order," said Hugh, who had been taking a quick look at the stores. "This doesn't make sense."

"The only people who knew we had such a radio were those *Windward* chaps; come to think of it, they were taking a long look at us, weren't they?"

"At teatime, yes," replied Hugh. "At least, one of them was."

"They must have watched us go down the road, and then one of them could have rowed across in their dinghy, and blown that valve; it wouldn't be a long job for anyone who knew his stuff ; especially if he had handled Services radio gear. Why on earth do a thing like that ? And how does this bit of card fit into the scheme of things ? It looks as if there's excitement ahead ! I wonder if I can get a replacement for that valve ? I'll have a try tomorrow."

" That is if they don't come across and fix an underwater charge to our hull during the night ! " added Hugh, brightly.

" This may be more serious than you think, Hugh. I am wondering if we ought to make a complaint to the police."

" I shouldn't do that ; we haven't any evidence against them, and we should look foolish if the police asked us for some hard facts. It's all suspicions so far. That card may have been left by the previous hirers of the boat, and just slipped out of its corner this evening. It might mean anything."

" What's that noise ? " suddenly interrupted John ; there was a touch of jumpiness in his voice. Then, with a sigh of relief, he went on : " Oh ! It must be the Vincent family, singing themselves to sleep ! "

## Chapter 6

### IN WHICH VIKING FINDS AN ALLY

FROM the direction of the *Sabrina* there came the sound of singing, accompanied by a softly-strummed stringed instrument.

"Somebody's playing a zither," explained Hugh. "I've heard one of them before. It's something like strumming the chords of a piano. I rather like it."

"It sounds very nice coming across the water," said John. "At any rate, it hasn't any valves to blow," he added ruefully.

"That's a hymn they're singing, isn't it?" asked Hugh.

"Yes; it sounds like one, though I don't know it myself. Yet it sounds familiar. . . . I know! They sang it after one of those beach services I was telling you about; I happened to be there that evening, and they gave me a hymn-sheet. The words were rather good, I thought. There was one verse which said something about ' Thy Church unsleeping, while earth rolls onward into night . . . er . . . her watch is keeping, and does not fail by day or night.' It was an evening hymn; and I remember thinking how impressive it was to sing it at sunset with the waves rolling in on the beach behind. It made you feel how small and insignificant you really are in comparison with the great truths of life."

" They certainly seem to be thorough in their Christianity on *Sabrina*," remarked Hugh. " But I must say I like what little I've seen of them, in spite of that ! "

" Now you're being unkind ! If the crew of *Windward* felt the same way as the Vincents, my radio would probably still be working properly."

" Don't you start preaching at me ; come on, it's time to brew cocoa and prepare for shut-eye ; we want to make an early start in the morning."

" Wait a moment ! " replied John. " I think I would like to have a word with our friends on *Sabrina* about our suspected mysterious visitor this evening. You can go ahead with the brew while I slip along and see what they have to say."

" Right-ho ; any other jobs you would like me to do ? I think I'd rather come along with you ; they seem to have stopped hymn-singing."

With that, Hugh followed John out through the door in the awning, on to the bank, and along to the *Sabrina*.

" Stop a moment," said John, looking in the direction of the porthole in the side of the cabin. " We can't butt in on this."

Hugh looked in the same direction, and could see Christine and Dick with their heads bowed in the attitude of prayer.

The two friends were just turning away when they heard Dick Vincent's voice, and saw a shaft of light caused by the sudden opening of the cabin door.

"Come on, Chris," Dick was saying. "We'll have some more of that super-special cocoa which you made last night ; I'll light the primus, and you can mix the dope."

It was obvious that the prayer-meeting, or whatever it had been, was over.

John and Hugh turned back again, jumped on board, and John cautiously put his head through the open flap of the awning, saying, " Excuse us barging in like this, but we wonder if you could spare us a moment or two. Something rather queer has happened."

" Why certainly," said Dick, " come right in ; mind the saucepan. Is anybody hurt ? "

" Nobody's hurt, but we felt we'd like some advice."

" Come into the cabin," said Dick. " Chris, old thing, I'm sure you would like to show these gentlemen how wonderfully you brew cocoa ; make an extra two gallons ! "

" Only if you promise to let me hear the news, especially if it's exciting," was the girl's reply.

" What's the commotion out there ? " said a deeper voice from the cabin ; then Mr. Vincent looked out enquiringly into the well.

" John and Hugh want some advice, Dad," explained Dick.

" We'll do what we can ; come into the cabin," said Mr. Vincent. " What's the trouble ? " he went on, as they settled themselves on the spring berths which ran along each side of the cabin.

John proceeded to relate what they had found on their return from the walk, and their suspicions as to the cause of the unexpected breakdown of the radio.

" Your suspicions certainly sound plausible," said Mr. Vincent ; " I rather agree with Hugh, however, that there isn't anything like enough to go on to justify approaching the police. Supposing we appoint ourselves honorary watchdogs for the next few days, and see if these fellows get up to any mischief ? What do you say, Dick ? "

" I'm game for anything like that, Father. Of course, we shall have to send Chris home ; we don't want anyone so delicate as she is to be mixed up in any bother," he added, mischievously.

" Delicate my foot ! " came the emphatic reply from the well, where the roaring of the primus had not prevented Chris from listening to the report which John had given. " If you had been in Chefoo with us during the war, instead of spending your days in luxury at school in the English countryside, you'd have something to talk about. The only hardship you have ever known was the night the prefect forgot to tuck your little toes-ies up in bed ! "

" All right, all right ! I'll withdraw that remark," said Dick cheerily. " But you'll have to put yourself under military discipline and do all that the First Mate tells you ; won't she, Dad ? "

" If the First Mate is involved, I should suspect that it would be Mercantile Marine discipline, not Military," chaffed Mr. Vincent. " In any case, I haven't decided which of you is to be First Mate, yet ; you're both working for your ticket still ! "

" Anyhow, I suggest we work together on this," continued John, in more serious tones. " We can easily arrange some pretext for having a talk in the morning, and we will stay here until we see which way *Windward* is moving. I really want to have a scout round for a spare valve tomorrow morning. There's an old R.A.F. depôt a little way from here, and I might find someone in charge of the stores who will take pity on me."

" Very well ; we'll see you again in the morning," said Mr. Vincent. " Good night."

" Good night everybody, Good night."

" Here, what about your cocoa ! " said Christine. " It's all ready now ! "

So they drank cocoa and talked awhile, and then slipped back to the *Viking* and were soon snugly tucked up in their bunks.

## Chapter 7

### JOHN CALLS IN THE R.A.F.

MONDAY morning dawned bright and clear with the promise of plenty of wind. Thin, ragged wisps fanned out from a very high bank of misty cloud, while lower in the sky there were a few scattered puffs of cumulous cloud which looked as if they would grow larger as the day wore on. John was up early (but not before the occupants of the *Windward*, he noticed), and arranged that Hugh should see the Vincents, and should try to come to an arrangement whereby they would follow *Windward*, whichever way she went, and leave some kind of note at Thurne Mouth, if she went back downstream, so that the *Viking* could follow on. John felt that if the crew of *Windward* were prepared to risk serious trouble in order to put his radio out of action, then it was worth his while going to some trouble to get it going again. He had a close friend who had served in the R.A.F. at a Radio-location Maintenance Depôt near Potter, Heigham during the war, and he had an idea that he might be able to get the replacement he needed. Without waiting for breakfast, he set off for the road.

A bus came along just as he reached it, and

he jumped thankfully on board. He was very soon at the point nearest the Depôt (the conductor gave him clear directions), and after walking down a very rough, cinder-covered lane, he found himself at the barbed-wire protected entrance to a collection of dismal-looking R.A.F. huts. Standing at the gate was a rather youthful corporal. John introduced himself, and told his story, without mentioning the suspicions that he held concerning the other yacht.

The corporal was interested. " You know, you're asking me to do something very, very naughty," he said, laughingly ; " but as it happens, I'm a keen amateur radio fan myself— though this job is doing its best to knock the keenness out of me ! I think I know how you feel. Look here, we've got a lot of that stuff lying derelict in the storeshed ; it's only going to be dumped. Hold on a little while, and I'll see what I can find. You did say it was a PMZX/44-C2, didn't you ? "

" That's right," said John, hopefully. " Or a PMZX/46-D1 would do."

The corporal disappeared, whistling cheerfully.

A few minutes later he returned, with a small packet in his hand.

" I think this one is O.K.," he said. " It came out of a set which had been damaged in a smash, and which had been put on the scrapheap ; but I gave it a quick test, and the filament is all right ; that's something."

"Thanks very much," said John. "How much do I owe you?"

"If I took money, it would be a serious offence; as it is, it came out of a pile of condemned junk, and you had better take it away as quickly as you can, with the good wishes of a fellow enthusiast.... And by the way," he went on, "when you get called up don't try to get into the wireless branch of the R.A.F.; you'll be bored stiff. Radio is a good hobby, but not a very good employment!"

John thanked him again, turned and waved as he came to a bend in the lane, and then settled down to a gentle trot back to Potter Heigham Bridge. He put the precious valve into a safe pocket, taking good care to ensure that it would receive no knocks on the way.

When he arrived at the bridge, he slipped into the stores to get a newspaper and one or two oddments which were wanted on board the *Viking*, and hurried to see what was happening to the boats. All three were at their moorings, although it was obvious that someone had been busy on *Windward*, for her mast had been lowered and was resting in the crutches at the stern, so that she was all ready to get through the low road bridge.

As John approached the *Viking*, he caught the smell of bacon frying, and hurried to see what Hugh had in store for him; he was feeling ravenously hungry after his early morning expedition. When he entered the cabin, he saw Dick Vincent sitting on one of the berths while Hugh was busy with the primuses.

"Well, John, how did you get on?" asked Hugh.

"I think I've got what I want; the valve hasn't been properly tested, but the chap there was very friendly, and he seemed to know his stuff."

"Jolly good show," said Dick. "Hugh tells me that you can transmit with your set: that should be interesting, because we've a small receiver on *Sabrina*; you will be able to call us up if you get lost!!"

"What about the pursuit of the *Windward*?" asked John. "Is everything fixed up?"

"Well," said Hugh, "it's obvious she's going under the bridge, since her mast is down. We can't lose her for a little while, because there's only one route she can take up to the end of Hickling Sound; and then she'll either have to go on to Hickling, or up to Horsey Mere. The tide is still running fast through the bridge here, so she's hardly likely to move off for another hour or so; we should not be very far behind."

"We've had breakfast," said Dick, "and Dad and Chris are getting the mast ready for lowering. I'm going aboard to give them a hand. We'll get away first, and keep fairly close to *Windward*, as we're not under direct suspicion. The only thing that worries us is how we can let you know which way she goes at the river junction. My father found out from a friend, before we came up here, that it is impossible to go straight up to West Somerton, as the swing bridge by Morgrove Hall is fast across the water, and can't be moved. So *Windward* must go up towards Hickling. The question is whether she'll go to Hickling or Horsey."

" I've an idea ! " said John. " What sort of radio is yours ? "

" Just a straightforward portable of the old type ; it's not a superhet ; I wish it was ; we might be able to separate the Home Service from Hilversum a bit better ! "

" Then you can make it oscillate ? "

" Not half ! "

" Right. When you see which way she is going, just turn up the reaction, make it whistle, and then switch on and off three times if she goes to Hickling, five if to Horsey. We'll be listening out just about the time you should reach there, and we'll know which way to come. Tune in on Hilversum I, then I'll know where to listen. Got the idea ? "

" Seems clear enough to me. I'll get back now, and help the others with the mast. I may say something rather ridiculous as I go out, but it will just be to calm any suspicious minds there may be about."

" Cheerio, then," he said, as he went outside. " Many thanks for the screwdriver. We may

see you again before the end of the week. I hope
you get your radio mended." All this was spoken
in a carefully loud tone, as he jumped on to the
bank.

Hugh rose to the occasion smartly.

"That's all right ; it was no trouble at all. I
don't suppose we shall bother very much about
the radio now ; not much chance of getting
spares in these parts."

Dick disappeared into the cabin of the *Sabrina*,
while Hugh and John, one of them keeping a
careful eye on *Windward*, tackled a tasty and
hearty breakfast.

## Chapter 8

### WINDWARD IS PURSUED

SOON after ten o'clock, *Windward* was un-moored, and the fair-headed member of her crew took the quant pole as he prepared to push her against the now slowing tide. John noted with satisfaction that the Vincents had lowered their mast, and were almost ready to move off.

Hugh watched the proceedings with interest, as he had not seen a Broads yacht go through one of the low bridges ; he noted the way in which *Windward* was skilfully navigated through, the man with the quant operating at the stern and then pushing with his hands against the brickwork as they went underneath. Then *Sabrina* followed, about a quarter-of-an-hour later ; Chris took the tiller (and seemed quite competent at it) while Mr. Vincent on one side, and Dick on the other, used their two quant poles to good effect. Both the boats continued quanting upstream, as there was a railway bridge beyond the road bridge, and this also was too low to be negotiated with the mast up.

" We had better get under way soon," said John ; " we'll give them a little start. It will help to dull any suspicions they may have."

He turned over the page of the newspaper which he had bought that morning.

" Anything happening ? " said Hugh.

" Nothing beyond what we heard last night on the radio. That reminds me, I must try out my new valve soon. I think I'll wait until we're through the bridge, though . . . I say, here's something interesting. It's about those jolly old agitators. There are three specially important ones, it appears. They seem to be smart and very dangerous types. . They are all wanted on charges of suspected sabotage. This paper says that there is strong suspicion that they are being helped by some sort of organization over here. You remember those men who were brought to trial last year for doing something similar. But these seem to be key-men, and there is no doubt they are trying to get back to Diamatia. They may have some secret information to carry. Watch is being kept at all East Coast ports. Special Branch men from Scotland Yard have been sent to the provinces to make further enquiries. They seem to be taking this very seriously, Hugh. They don't normally make all this fuss about such types."

" It would be some ' do ' if they tried to steal the *Viking* from us, and sail across the North Sea in it ! The snag being, of course, that they would have to carry it some miles over land ; I've just been looking at the map, and this river comes to a dead end along here, about three miles from the sea."

" But they *could* get out to sea, Hugh ; you can go down the Bure to Yarmouth, and then instead of turning inland again through Breydon Water to Norwich, you can go straight out to sea past Gorleston.  Barges often come that way from the Thames |to Norwich ; I believe small coasting vessels do the trip with coal."

" Yes, but you wouldn't get far across the North Sea in this craft, surely ? "

" No, you wouldn't, especially at this time of the year.  But you do get sea-going craft on the Broads.  The *Windward*, for instance ; she's more sturdily built, and I shouldn't be surprised if she hasn't an extra-heavy keel that will fit her for sea navigation.  That would also explain the transmitter we think she has on board."

" John !  I've got it !  Supposing she is something to do with those wanted men !  She might belong to the organization which is helping them ; perhaps she's going to slip through Yarmouth with the three Diamatians on board ! She could transfer them to another ship out at sea, and then return in all her innocence as a pleasure yacht ! "

" Sounds fantastic to me, Hugh.  But it's quite an idea.  What's she doing up here though ?  If she's got a trio of desperadoes on board, she doesn't want to waste time showing them the beauties of Broadland."

" No, I suppose not.  Still, you never know. I wonder what that little card we found is all about. Perhaps they'll twig that it was dropped on board here, and make another raid on our cabin."

" That's not so likely ; I guess it isn't the only copy ; and in any case it makes sheer nonsense to folk like ourselves. Anyhow, we must get moving. You finish clearing away, and I'll get everything set for lowering the mast."

John opened up the " tabernacle," checked up to see that the base of the mast could swing upwards without fouling any of the gear, and then unshackled the gaff and boom and laid them on one side so that they would not hinder the lowering. Eventually he called Hugh to take his post in the well, and take the weight of the mast as it came down to the crutches.

" Better put the low crutches in," he added, after giving his other instructions. " I've seen a mast badly scraped by someone forgetting that little detail when they went through this bridge. You see how marked the brickwork is ; we don't want to leave that sort of mark on Broadland ! "

Eventually all was ready. John unfastened the heavy galvanized steel bar which kept the foot of the mast in position, and then, taking part of the strain with his foot on the lower end of the mast, he began to pay out the halyard which loosened the forestay. Gradually the mast swung backwards, until Hugh, standing on the seats in the well, was able to take the greater part of the strain, and lower it into place in the

crutches. It was then only a few moments' work
to get the anchors, and start quanting upstream
towards the bridge. When they reached the
narrow, tunnel-like opening, there was still a fair
current flowing, and John had to strain hard at
the quant pole in order to keep *Viking* moving.
As soon as they had pushed the bows out on the
other side, the pressure eased, however, and with
one good push against the brickwork itself
*Viking* was moving smoothly towards the railway
bridge. Here there was no narrow arch, and
they were soon moored upstream of the railway,
by the starboard bank.

"I'm going to try the radio out," said John;
"we may get the signal from the Vincents soon.
I wonder whether you could go back to the yard
on some pretext, and see if you can find out
anything about *Windward*. Give me a hand
with the mast first, and then I can rig my aerial."

"Good idea; I'll try to get some paraffin, and
see what I can learn," said Hugh. "Up with
the mast then!"

After one or two false lifts, due to the stays
catching on the side of the cabin-roof ("You
always get that trouble," said John), they
quickly had the mast in its proper position, and
Hugh trotted back to the boatyard with the
spare paraffin can.

John busied himself with his radio, and found,
to his delight, that it was working. He tried a
quick turn round the short-wave dial, but there

was no activity on the wavelengths on which they had heard the mysterious stations of the day before.  He turned it over to the medium-wave band and left it switched on at the Hilversum wavelength.  A rather pleasant programme of light music was being broadcast, and he left it playing softly whilst he prepared to hoist sail. He had the jib laid out ready on the foredeck, the mainsail with its peak halyard shackled on correctly, and was giving the cabin a much-needed clean-up, when Hugh returned, somewhat out of breath after his hundred-yard trot. " Did you get what you wanted ? " he asked.

" Yes and No ! " was the reply.  " No paraffin —at least not from the yard ; I had to go to the stores for some—but a little information which strikes me as very interesting."

" What's that ? " asked John, impatiently.

" Well, I got into conversation with the fellow at the boatyard, saying what a handsome craft the *Windward* was, and he said. . . ."

" Keep quiet a minute ! " interrupted John, sharply.

Hugh was about to protest at this sudden change of interest, when he realized what was happening.

Over and above the music of the William Tell Overture, which Hilversum was broadcasting just then, there came a piercing whistle, which varied in pitch as the person responsible for it turned the tuning control of his set.   Whee-ee-ee (upwards now)—pause—whee-ee-ee (down-wards again). " Something like an Air Raid Warning ! " observed Hugh, helpfully.

" Shut up, and listen ! " retorted John, " here comes the signal ! "

The wailing signal ceased ; the whistle stopped momentarily. Then came the signal ; five suc-cessive dashes, followed by a further period of howling ascents and descents.

" So it's Horsey," said John. " That's about the most deserted stretch of all ; there's usually some first-rate sailing up there, especially at this time of year when the weeds have died down. I think the sooner we start sailing now, the better. But I've forgotten your information ; what did you learn ? "

" The skipper of the *Windward* has been known around here for many years ; he has a bungalow at Horning. He had some sort of mystery job during the war, so it was said, and disappeared for the greater part of it. His yacht is a sea-going craft ; he used to specialize in voyages across the North Sea to the North German ports before the war. She's just been fitted with a new set of sails, and is fairly fast, though her sturdy build slows her down a little. The man said that he had heard that she had made one or two short journeys out to sea this summer, but couldn't go far because of the minesweeping still going on. I had to stop asking questions then, otherwise they might have thought my curiosity rather suspicious."

" Hm," said John, thoughtfully. " Voyages to the North German ports, eh ? Doesn't sound too good, in view of your suggestion, Hugh."

" We certainly shan't be able to follow him quite that far ! " replied Hugh. " But if we do get some definite evidence against him we can ring the police at Yarmouth and get him stopped ; he must go out that way."

" Yes, but the job now is to follow him and see if he gets up to any mischief. Stand by to set sails ! "

## *Chapter* 9

### VIKING WINS A RACE

SOON the white wings of the *Viking* were unfurled in the now steady breeze, and John sent her scudding along northwards as speedily as he could. At times the wind blew vigorously, and *Viking* leaned over gracefully, yielding to the unseen pressure, and drawing from it power which sent her steadily on.

John had fetched the little white card, and was puzzling over it as he steered. Hugh was preparing vegetables for dinner, between intervals of surveying the scenery, which was not very interesting at this point. They quickly reached the point where Heigham Sound branched off to port. As they swung round on to the other tack, they found that the going was not quite so straightforward, and as the channel wound its way through the reeds which covered what had once been a large open stretch of water, they found it necessary to change from one tack to the other—an operation which was none too easy in the narrow waterway. But Hugh enjoyed the continual movement, the hectic dashes across the channel, the steady turns at each change, the feel of vibrant power as *Viking's* sails filled with wind on each new tack, and thrust her towards the opposite bank.

When they came to the point at which Meadow Dyke led off towards Horsey Mere, John suggested that they should moor for a short while, and eat a light lunch, saving their heavier meal for the evening. This they did, nosing the *Viking* into a clump of reeds, where, snugly moored up, they brewed a quick cup of tea, and ate sandwiches. They did not stay long over their meal. Both were anxious to follow up the *Windward*, and they soon cast off, crossing Heigham Sound towards Meadow Dyke. As they did so, John observed a swirl of mud in their wake.

" We're touching bottom across here," he said ; " I hope it doesn't get too shallow, or we'll be stuck fast ; and with this wind behind us, we should be glued down well and truly. I'm keeping close to the guide posts, but some of these Broads channels are badly silted up, and you can never quite tell what to expect."

*Viking* suddenly felt sluggish ; she no longer responded freely to the urge of the wind ; the dark trail thickened ominously behind her. Suddenly, however, she felt free again, and was gliding into Meadow Dyke, the very narrow channel which led to Horsey Mere.

Here the water was crystal clear, and they amused themselves watching the young fish which abounded in the stream as they darted to and fro among the decaying brown and green weeds. On the bottom of the Dyke they could see occasional traces of previous passers-by, in

the form of empty tins and cardboard boxes.
The dyke twisted and turned, but the wind was
steadily favourable, and they got through without
having to change tack—which would have been
almost impossible.

" There's a yacht moored up ahead," said
Hugh, suddenly catching sight of a mast rising
above the reeds in front of them.

" Must be *Windward* or *Sabrina*," said John ;
" I doubt if there are any others about round
here at this time of the year."

" Well, we can't stop or go back, even if it is
the *Windward*," said Hugh, " so put on your most
innocent look and keep sailing."

" You take her over for a minute," said
John, quickly, " I'm going to disappear into
the cabin. Steer for that duck-shooting shelter
over there ; she'll keep on the present tack if
you aim straight." With that, he went into the
cabin.

Hugh took the *Viking* on the stated course,
passing fairly near the *Windward*, and observing
its skipper sitting in the well, reading a newspaper. Across the broad stretch of Horsey Mere,
somewhat to his right, he could see another
yacht cruising rather aimlessly along ; this
seemed to be *Sabrina* ; no other craft was in sight.
Horsey Mere itself was a picture of wild beauty,
with its clumps of bronze-tinted trees, its duck-
shooting boxes, made of timber and reeds, and
its general air of loneliness. Across to the north-

east, Hugh could see the bare branches of the trees where, so he had read, the sea had broken through the sand-dune defences some years previously, killing off all growth in the area which it flooded, and affecting even the wild life in Horsey itself.

When they had sailed about half-way across the Broad, John came out of the cabin, with a look of excitement on his face.

" More mystery ! " he said. " You saw that newspaper which the skipper of the *Windward* was reading ? "

" Well, I thought I would take a good look at her through the telescope ; that's why I went below ; I pointed it through one of the portholes, hiding it as best I could with the curtain, and had a good long look at her. The interesting thing was that newspaper ; it was the *Daily Telegraph,* and it was quite out of date ; I remember the picture on the front page ; it was of that big fire in the oil wells in America ; do you remember ?     It certainly wasn't today's or Saturday's, for they have quite different pictures. If I remember rightly it was about a week or ten days ago.   You couldn't mistake that black cloud of smoke.   I wonder what they want with an old *Daily Telegraph* ? "

" Probably doing the crossword," suggested Hugh.   " Anyhow, you can't have a chap arrested for reading an old newspaper.   Though I do think that some of those who write them

could do with a short spell in clink ; the trash
they turn out ! "

By now the *Viking* was half-way across Horsey
Mere, sailing swiftly through the clear water,
heading for a mooring near *Sabrina*.

" We must have another council-of-war soon,"
said John.  " I expect we can arrange to meet
so that the *Windward* crew don't see us ; it will
be as well not to show our relationship too
obviously.  At the same time we don't want to
let *Windward* out of our sight if we can help it."

*Sabrina* was still cruising across the north-
eastern end of the Mere, about half a mile away
from *Windward*, and John contrived to steer
*Viking* within easy hailing distance, without
making it look too deliberate.

Remembering how sounds carry across water,
he spoke in a comparatively low voice to Dick
Vincent, who was at the tiller of *Sabrina*.

" Everything in order ? " he asked.

" Yes ; nothing to cause further suspicion.
What about you ? "

John gave him a quick outline of the discoveries which Hugh had made at the boatyard
and then added :

" I think the best thing we can do is to moor
up in that channel in the north-east corner, and
discuss things further.  If one of us stays in
sight of the *Windward*, it will be enough.  You
go a little farther up towards Horsey staithe,
and we'll keep watch ; then you can come down

to us in your dinghy, and we can lay plans."

"Suits me," said Dick. "But it's very early yet to moor up ; can't we have a race ? That won't make them suspicious ; everybody races on the Broads, whether they know one another or not. Let's make our course round the three duck-shooting ' hides ' ; we'll start level at that one nearest the *Windward*, and go right round the Mere. We'll take our jib down to make things fairer if you like ! ! "

"You won't, boastful ! You'll be hanging your handkerchiefs out to get a bit more drive before we've finished with you ! "

John called Hugh to " action stations," told him of the challenge, and manœuvred *Viking* steadily towards the starting-point.

The course would take them roughly in a triangle. The start would be at the lower apex of the Mere, near *Windward's* mooring, then there would be one leg with the wind almost dead aft, a second with the wind on the port beam, and a third driving almost straight into it. They were tacking now, covering what would be part of the third leg of the race. John was busy watching *Sabrina* as she came down nearer them, trying to see if he could spot any weaknesses in the handling of the now rival vessel. Dick was at the tiller ; Mr. Vincent was with him in the well, and Chris was lying on the foredeck, ready to help " weather " the jib if necessary. John could see the advantages of

6

having someone in her position, especially as there was still some risk of getting caught in clumps of decaying weed, which could be avoided with the help of a look-out. He eventually made up his mind.

"Will you go for'ard, Hugh?" he asked. "I'll try and manage here on my own, and you can keep your eye open for trouble ahead. It's none too deep in places. You can be ready to lend a hand with the jib if necessary."

Both yachts were now sailing almost side by side, on the starboard tack, ready to swing over on to the port tack as they turned round the square, reed-protected shooting box.

Their first attempt was not successful; *Viking* had an undoubted advantage as they turned to start, and so they agreed to go back and try again.

The crew of the *Windward* were making no attempt to hide their interest, and were both in the well of their boat, looking on.

Then came the surprise. *Sabrina* and *Viking* had turned completely round, and were just passing *Windward* on their way to their second attempt at a start, when her skipper hailed them. He spoke in a cultured, English voice.

"May we join in your race, please? We couldn't help overhearing your remarks as you came past, and we would like to try our little craft against yours. We can get under way in a few moments."

John looked across at Dick; it was impossible

to say anything of what they felt, as they would have been overheard.

" By all means ! " said John. " We'll hang on, while you hoist sail."

" Thanks ; there aren't many craft about at this time of the year, and it's usually a job to find an opponent," said the *Windward* skipper, pleasantly.

John and Dick took their respective boats round in a wide circle. When they were some distance away, Dick spoke as softly as he could. The wind was rising somewhat, so that it was not easy to make oneself understood without shouting.

" Bit of a nuisance," he said. " But we'll have to put up with it. It will give us some idea of his sailing qualities ; that's one good thing ! "

" Yes, but it will tell him the same about us, which is not so good. However, we must go through with it now. I suggest we combine forces if necessary to make sure he doesn't win. Anyhow, we'll see how we go."

By now *Windward* had cast off, and was sailing round on a course which would bring her alongside the other two.

" Going to be somewhat crowded with three of us," said John to Hugh. " Especially if we are together at any of the turns."

Now the three yachts were practically level as they approached the first marking-point. John called across the details of the course to the

*Windward*, and then they were ready for the start. They turned upwind, and passed the shooting-box almost exactly level. Immediately they leaped ahead, with the now strong breeze behind them, and their sails bellying out, filled with wind. *Sabrina* was obviously the fastest on this stretch, and began to pull slowly ahead, with *Viking* and *Windward* ploughing along, neck and neck, a short way behind. Suddenly John called Hugh back from the bows.

"Take over for a while, will you ? I've just noticed something ! Keep her on the present course ; I'll be with you by the time we reach the first turn."

With that John disappeared hurriedly into the cabin. Hugh, thrilled with the experience of sailing *Viking* on his own in such a breeze, hung on grimly to the fiercely-tugging mainsheet, and weighed against the tiller as he held her on a straight course. By now *Windward* had crept a little ahead of *Viking*, with *Sabrina* still going away from them both ; she was obviously the fastest of the three when the wind was aft. Sighing and moaning across the reeds it came, bending them low, and whipping crests of foam off the tops of the waves. Hugh could not help wondering what had made John disappear so quickly, but was not going to quarrel with a decision which left him in charge. He could give *Viking* no more sail, so he concentrated on keeping her as steady as he could, though at times it was impossible to resist the swing as an extra-powerful gust of wind pulled her slightly off her course. He noticed that the skipper of the *Windward* had also left the other member of his crew in charge, and was out of sight.

They were getting near the turn when John emerged from the cabin, a look of triumph on his face.

" I'll tell you all about it later," he said, " I'm sure that *Windward* crew are up to some mischief ; she's just been transmitting another code message. But now the race is the thing ; you've been letting me down, I see ! "

" Sorry, sir," mocked Hugh. " I've kept her as you left her ; I'm afraid the others are just a bit too fast for us. Perhaps we shall pick up on the next stretch."

John took over again, and Hugh went forward to his station on the forepeak, observing as he did so that the skipper of the *Windward* had also come back to the tiller of his craft.

Now *Sabrina* was turning into the second leg of the triangle and made a graceful picture as she swung on to the other tack, heeled hard over as the wind caught her on the beam, and settled down for the cross-wind stretch of the course. Dick Vincent's face wore a triumphant air as he looked back at his pursuers ; *Windward* was second round the mark, closely followed by *Viking*. On this section, the two hindermost began to catch up very slowly ; *Windward* especially, drawing away from *Viking* and nearer to *Sabrina*; her heavier build and no doubt heavier keel, designed for sea-going, helped her here, enabling her to take full advantage of the strong beam wind. *Sabrina* tended to drift sideways if Dick held her mainsheet down too hard. *Viking* also caught up somewhat on the leader, so that the three yachts were more closely bunched as they went into the next turn, and prepared for the hardest stretch of all, the long beat against the wind to the finishing point.

On this last stretch, where they had to tack all the way, there was the fullest opportunity for skill and yachtsmanship to reveal themselves. It soon appeared that the *Windward* had the measure of both the others; she turned with real smartness at the end of each board, and gained at each turn. She was also able to sail closer to the wind than *Sabrina*, though no closer than *Viking*. The look of triumph on Dick Vincent's face changed to one of anxiety and concern as *Windward* slowly overtook him, and *Viking* began to draw up. The three yachts had now become somewhat split up as they made their individual tacks to and fro, but there was no question of *Windward's* lead. John had reconciled himself to fighting it out with Dick for second place when Hugh shouted back to him.

" I think we're gaining a little ! "

John kept a careful eye on the leader, and sure

enough as they both turned on a fresh tack *Viking* was closer. *Sabrina* was still a short way behind. With fresh hope, John threw himself into the struggle, straining every nerve to gain on his rival. He swung *Viking* into each successive turn with a furious abandon, exulting in the splash of the spray as it came back over the bows, and concentrating all his attention on squeezing the last ounce of thrust out of his sails.

Slowly *Viking* crept up, until, greatly daring, John turned short on one tack and cut across in front of *Windward*. Two more tacks, and then it was a straight run for the finishing mark. Holding grimly on to his short lead, with *Windward* pressing him hard, sailing close behind him, slightly to port, John drove the *Viking* mercilessly past the shooting-box, his face all smiles, and a shout of " Done it ! " on his lips.

Dick Vincent waved to him from his position in the rear, and the skipper of the *Windward* was all smiles as they prepared to turn and ease off.

It was then that the disaster occurred ; suddenly, and unexpectedly. John was looking ahead, taking care not to run on to the reeds, and preparing to turn north-eastwards again. He put the tiller hard over, planning to complete the circle, and so bring *Viking* to a standstill opposite the entrance to Meadow Dyke.

" Look out," shouted Hugh, from the bows. " Mind the *Windward* ! "

It was too late.

The skipper of the *Windward*, who had turned slightly to port, was apparently busy adjusting something in the well of his yacht. The result was that, as *Viking* turned, she became broadside on to *Windward*, which, sailing still on the course on which she had finished the race, was travelling fast.

" Look out ! " yelled John ; the *Windward's* skipper looked up again, and did his best to avoid a collision, but in vain.

The stoutly - built stem of the *Windward* crunched into the side of the *Viking*. There was an ugly splintering sound, a violent jerk, and then both yachts righted themselves as they parted, each helmsman having taken avoiding action.

*(See Frontispiece for illustration)*

## Chapter 10

### JOHN BECOMES A SUPERNUMERARY

THE blow had apparently caught the *Viking* at a weak spot, crushing in part of the hull and the deck. The damage could not be properly assessed while they were sailing, and John quickly ran her alongside the bank, where Hugh jumped out and moored her.

The *Windward* had turned a complete circle, and gone back to her former mooring, where she had been before she joined the race. As soon as she was tied up, her skipper came across in his dinghy to where John and Hugh, now joined by Dick and Chris Vincent, were surveying the damage.

" I'm terribly sorry," he said, as he came near. " I do hope that it isn't too serious. I don't want to spoil your holiday ! "

" That's all right, you couldn't help it. I'm afraid we shall have to get some first-aid repairs done, as the cabin will leak rather badly if it rains. However, I don't think the main timbers are affected, and we cannot see any damage below the water line. We've had a quick look under the floor-boards."

" I'm fully covered by my insurance," said the *Windward's* skipper, " including racing mishaps, and as I'll take all the blame you should

not suffer any loss. I suggest that the best
thing would be for you to get back to Potter
Heigham, ring the owners at Horning, and see if
they will give you permission to get temporary
repairs done at Potter ; that will save your
having to go all the way back to your starting-
point."

"Yes, I think you're right," said John.
"Perhaps we had better exchange particulars
right away, and then we can leave the insurance
companies to fight it out."

He took out a notebook from his pocket,
scribbled his name and address on a spare leaf,
and gave it to the other. The man from the
*Windward* dictated his name and address, John
writing it down as follows : "Captain Bruce
Craven, Slavonia ('That's the name of my
bungalow,' he explained), Horning."

After further profuse apologies, and an offer
of help, which John politely declined, Captain
Craven made his way back to his yacht, which,
having taken the force of the collision at her
strongest point, was practically undamaged.

Dick Vincent climbed aboard the *Viking* to
help its crew make a thorough check of the
damage.

"I'm not so sure that was an accident, you
know," he ventured.

"What do you mean ? "

"Well, I was watching friend Craven rather
carefully on that last stretch ; he was pulling

away from you quite easily ; there's no doubt his is the fastest of the three when it comes to beating against the wind. Then, suddenly, you began to catch up. You were probably congratulating yourselves on your achievement, and concentrating on completing his defeat ; but I thought that he was deliberately slowing, and dragging his turns. I didn't see any reason why you should have begun to gain on him like that ; it so puzzled me that I looked rather more carefully at him, and I am certain he was holding back a little. Then, when he was in a nice position to ram you, he bent down to do some job or other in the well. All that I can say is that if he had tried to do it deliberately and make it look like an accident, he couldn't have done it better ! Now he has very neatly put you out of action for a day or two. Not suspecting that we are working together, he probably thinks he has got rid of the trouble-maker."

" Well I'm dashed ! " exclaimed John. " I never thought of that ! But perhaps you're right. Now I can add my little piece. Just after we had started, I noticed that Captain Craven went into his cabin. It seemed strange that he should leave just as the race was beginning, so I thought I would check up on things. I slipped down and turned my radio on, and there, sure enough, was that mystery transmitter, which I now think is on the *Windward*, going for all it was worth. It was another code message, and I've taken it down in full ; just a succession of numbers, however. It doesn't make any sense."

" I'm getting more and more convinced that he's mixed up with these wanted agitator-blokes," added Hugh. " Where should he be trans-mitting to, if not to Diamatia ? And why should he be so desperately anxious to get us out of the way ? He tried to transmit his message whilst we were engrossed in the race, and then took advantage of the opportunity to knock us out of his way. If you ask me, he is both clever and ruthless ; a really nasty piece of work."

" If what you're saying is right," said Dick, " then we're getting mixed up in something big. Can't we cheat him yet ? "

" I  know ! " interrupted John, hurriedly. " We'll surprise him in spite of this mess. We'll take *Viking* back to Potter Heigham, as he so thoughtfully suggested, but I don't see why both her crew need go as well. We'll sail her a little way down Meadow Dyke, and then I'll jump out, hide among the reeds, with my radio, and you can pick me up a little later. If the *Wind-ward* should come first, I'll lie doggo."

" That's all right ; but what about me ? " asked Hugh.

" You can hang on at Potter Heigham and try to get the boat patched up there. We're bound to come down that way soon, especially if the *Windward* is going to make a dash for the North

Sea ; there's no other way out. If I want to get a message to you, I can send a telegram to the Post Office, to be called for."

" I can't say I'm very excited about that plan. I'll tell you what ! Let's change both the radio sets over ; then you can transmit and talk to me from *Sabrina* ; maybe you'll find it useful to have an ally at Potter Heigham. If things get really hot, I can get the police ; you're miles from anywhere up here."

" Good idea ! I suggest we get under way as soon as possible ; it's teatime now, and we ought to make it look as if we're getting back to Potter by dusk. We've only an hour and a half to go, but you may just do it. We'll sail off in the normal way, Dick ; I'll drop off at the first convenient patch of reeds ; you can then follow a little later, pick me up, and return to keep an eye on Captain Craven and Co. ; O.K.? "

" Suits me," said Dick ; " I'll get back and explain things to Chris and Dad." He trotted back to *Sabrina*, returning shortly afterwards with two bundles, one of which was obviously a loaf of bread ; the other looked like one under its covering. In fact, it was their miniature radio. " There's something to keep you from starving," he said in a loud voice, for the *Windward's* benefit. " I hope you'll get back all right. Cheerio ! "

" Thanks a lot. Good-bye ! "

John and Hugh quickly set sail, and began the

tricky passage of the narrow Meadow Dyke
which led back toward Heigham Sound. The
wind had swung round to the East as the sun sank
lower, so that they did not have to tow their
craft out, as they had expected. At times it
was touch and go, as they sailed as close as possible
to the wind, but they scraped through the first
stretch (which was the worst), and were soon
rounding the bend into what would be an easier
section.

Here there was a clump of tall reeds reaching
to the river edge, and John, having issued a
stream of last-minute instructions to the in-
experienced Hugh, nosed *Viking* into the bank
and jumped ashore. Hugh then handed the
rather bulky radio set out to him, together with
one of the accumulators, and quickly moved off
downstream. They were now out of sight of the
*Windward*, but they did not want to cause
suspicion by stopping too long, as the top of
their mast might well be visible on the Mere.

John gave Hugh a helping shove off the bank,
watched him slipping away down the narrow
channel, and then hid himself among the reeds,
waiting for *Sabrina*. He could just see the tip
of her mast above the tall reeds, about two
hundred yards away, and watched anxiously
for the first sign of a move. All was quiet now
among the reeds, except for a steady murmur as
the breeze, now dropping slightly, touched and
bent their supple stems. The sun was growing

larger and redder as the day drew near to its close, and John could not help thinking that the *Windward's* crew had certainly chosen an ideal area for any tricks they had in mind. Wild, desolate, in places almost inaccessible except by water ; here men could be hidden, tragedies occur, all unknown to the outside world. An occasional cry from one of the wild birds which made their home around the fringes of the Mere only served to emphasize the eeriness of it all.

John's reverie was interrupted by signs of movement on *Sabrina* ; the tip of her mast began to move slowly towards him, and he prepared to show himself. She came towards him with some difficulty, not finding it so easy as the *Viking* to sail very close to the wind. Several times Dick Vincent had to give a heave on the quant pole in order to prevent her from losing way and being blown sideways into the bank. Eventually they arrived, John gave a quiet whistle, and, after looking round carefully, stepped out, handed his radio over to Dick in the well, and followed quickly. Straight into the cabin he went, there to remain as long as they were anywhere near *Windward*.

Then *Sabrina* turned round, and sailed easily back to Horsey Mere, passing *Windward* near the entrance. Captain Craven looked curiously at Dick and Chris as they steered her past. Dick had a further brainwave.

"Very difficult sailing against the breeze," he shouted across in a friendly fashion. "There's no room to manœuvre in that narrow channel ; looks as if we shall have to stay up here for the night ! "

"Yes, it is tricky work," came back the reply ; "I hope *Viking* makes it all right."

"She should do ; she seems able to sail closer to the wind than we can."

"She's pretty fast, taken all round. I'm sorry we gave her that knock ; they should be able to get it patched up at Potter."

"I hope so."

By now the distance between them made talking difficult, so Dick finished off the conversation with a cheerful "Good-night," and continued to sail towards the centre of the Mere.

Leaving *Sabrina* in his sister's charge, he then went below for a further consultation with his father and with John, who had been busy connecting up his radio, making it ready for use.

"I suggest we moor up nearby for the night, and talk things over thoroughly," said John, as they settled down to review their plans. "I can't help feeling that Hugh's suggestion was right, and that they've got something to do with these wretched Diamatians. If that's the case, they will probably make for the desolate area up what is called the New Cut ; it's an old disused canal which runs out of the north-west corner of the Mere, and leads to some really wild countryside, not far from the sand-dunes. I suggest that we moor up near the entrance to the Cut, and keep a watch all night in case they try to slip past in the dark. If they stay on the Mere, we shall see them in the morning ; and if they go down stream they must go to Potter Heigham, where Hugh will see them. The only other place they could go to is Hickling, and they would not have bothered to come up here if they had a rendezvous there. When we get moored up, we can go over all the facts we've unearthed so far, and see if we can make more sense of them."

"Good idea," said Mr. Vincent ; " I'll take over from Christine, while she brews some tea ; by the time we're moored, she'll just about have it ready ; I must say I can do with it ! "

With that, he and Dick went out into the well, from which Chris came into the cabin, and set to work in the tiny galley which occupied a narrow space between the cabin and the well, on the port side. Soon the primus was giving out its healthy roar, while John busied himself making certain that his radio was working well. He had arranged with Hugh that if some desperate need arose, Hugh could send him a morse message by oscillating the Vincents' set. In order to save batteries, they had agreed on set times for such messages, if they had to be sent : 2 p.m., 6 p.m., and 10 p.m., and 6 a.m. and

10 a.m.  He had also arranged that he would try to ring Hugh up at the Potter Heigham Bridge Stores call box at 9 a.m. and 4 p.m., though he could also transmit a radio message at the times agreed on for radio contact.  They had both realized, however, that they should avoid using the radio unless absolutely necessary.  Having lulled the *Windward's* crew into a sense of security, they did not want to spoil the effect.

John felt a gentle bump as *Sabrina* came to a standstill, and, looking through the porthole, saw that they had moored just at the entrance to a narrow channel, which he took to be the New Cut.  " Won't the *Windward* crowd be mad if they are really planning to come up here !" he thought to himself.  If he could have heard the comments of Captain Craven as he watched the manœuvre through his field-glasses, his worst fears would have been fully confirmed !

## Chapter 11

### A SECRET WEAPON PLAYS ITS PART

THE cabin of the *Sabrina* would have presented a cosy enough picture to any stranger who happened to look in at the conference which followed supper. Dick and John leaned back on the spring berths on one side, while Chris and her father settled themselves comfortably amidst piles of blankets on the other. The table was covered with a clean white cloth, and a gleaming coffee-pot held pride of place in the centre. The contents of this latter gave off a pleasant aroma, which completed the sense of relaxation and contentment.

But a few minutes spent listening to the conversation would soon have changed the opinion of our imaginary onlooker as to the mood of those present. Suggestion and counter-suggestion, theory and objection, followed one another in quick succession.

" Let's go back to the beginning, and see exactly how much we know," broke in Mr. Vincent, as John and Dick entangled themselves fiercely in a discussion about the code signals which John had heard transmitted. " Apparently *Windward* has some kind of hide-away between Horning and St. Benet's Abbey. She passed you on Saturday night, and yet she was behind you again on Sunday morning, although you saw no sign of her.  That's oddity number one."

"And the second is the radio business," interrupted John.  "It's pretty obvious that she has a powerful transmitter on board, although Captain Craven suggested otherwise in our little chat yesterday afternoon.  She also receives messages from a distant transmitter which uses the same call-sign, two dots followed by two dashes.  All the other messages are in some kind of numerical code.  If we could solve that, we'd know all we wanted to !"

"The third hard fact," added Dick, "is that she crashed into *Viking* this afternoon, in what seemed to me to be suspicious circumstances."

"Of course, the big advantage Captain Craven has," suggested Mr. Vincent, "is that he has a plan, and knows what he wants to do ; whereas we're doing a great deal of guesswork, and have to grope our way along."

"Yes," said Dick, "but it isn't all one-sided ; he now thinks that the *Viking* is out of the way ; he also imagines that her radio is out of action, in any case.  What he doesn't know is that John and his radio are both very much in the running still, and that *Sabrina* has taken up the scent.  There's nothing more dangerous than a false sense of security.  The big question, to my mind, is whether we ought not to call in the police right away.  I've read something about these foreigners myself ; there's no doubt that they are really dangerous specimens. If they can get back to Diamatia, they will cause no end of trouble for somebody."

" I don't think *Windward* has them on board yet," remarked Chris.

" Why not ? "

" Well, she wouldn't have messed about racing us round Horsey Mere. It would have been good policy to lie as low as possible if she had the fugitives in her cabin. Perhaps she has come out to this wild part in order to pick them up ; they wouldn't dare show themselves even at a place like Potter Heigham. But if they could be hidden away up here somewhere, *Windward* could pick them up quietly, and then slip out through Yarmouth."

" You've got something there, Chris," said Dick. " And if that's the case, our best policy is to appear innocent, and see if we can discover where the rendezvous is ; we can always ring through to Yarmouth, and get her stopped if they try to make a getaway. Perhaps we can leave the police out of it a little longer. We might, after all, be completely wrong ; I've heard of some strange mistakes being made on stronger evidence than we have."

" Don't you think these code messages are what we should concentrate on ? " suggested Mr. Vincent. " If we can get something out of them, we may have all the evidence we need."

"I think you're right," agreed John. "Before we get down to them again, one of us should take a peep outside to see if there's any sign of life from the *Windward*. She may try to slip past. We ought to get our watch set soon. If Captain Craven knows his way around the Broads as well as we think he does, he won't find any difficulty in sailing up here in the dark. I'll pop out and see how they're getting on."

Dick switched out the light to prevent the opening of the cabin door being betrayed to any watcher across the Mere, and John disappeared into the darkness. When he opened the canvas flap at the rear of the awning, he paused for a few moments to accustom his eyes to the darkness, and then looked carefully around.

Across to his left were the lights of a few cottages near Horsey staithe. All else was darkness, save for a dim light, apparently shining through a porthole, from where he estimated *Windward* would be. Everything appeared to be quiet, but he stayed a little while on deck to make sure there was no movement. Then he cautiously stepped ashore.

In *Sabrina's* cabin the Vincents were bent over a few scraps of paper, on which Hugh and John had written those parts of the mysterious code messages which they had recorded.

Suddenly Chris interrupted. "Let's use the secret weapon," she said. "John will be outside for a little while yet."

Dick and Mr. Vincent nodded agreement, and, without any further explanation, for they all seemed to know what Christine was referring to, they bowed their heads, and waited for a moment in silence. Then Dick began to pray, speaking quite naturally, and yet with a definite note of reverence in his voice.

" Lord, Thou knowest all about this problem ; we do pray that Thou wilt prevent our making any mistake, and if these should be the dangerous men we think they are, then help us to bring them to justice. Give us wisdom and understanding beyond our natural gifts. Help us also to witness for Thee to our new friend, that he may learn something of Thee, and desire Thee because of what he has seen in us. Amen."

" Amen," echoed Chris and her father, softly.

Then Mr. Vincent added a few words of prayer, followed by Chris, who referred especially to the effect which his stay with them would have upon John.

She had hardly finished when the cabin door quietly opened. For a moment, John stood there, looking on the strange scene. Then Chris looked up, her face broke into a natural smile, without a trace of awkwardness, and she asked :

" Well, John, did you see anything ? We've just been applying our secret weapon to the whole business."

It was John's turn to look a little awkward.

"Well, er, no ; that is, nothing suspicious. But we shall have to keep a continual watch from now on ; it will take the *Windward* only five minutes or so to get across the Mere to us, and we don't want them to slip past us unnoticed."

"It looks as if it may be an all-night business," remarked Mr. Vincent, thoughtfully. "I suggest that Chris takes the first watch, and then the three members of the so-called stronger sex can divide up the night between them."

"Good idea, Dad," was Chris's cheerful response. "I'll get my coat on, and I suggest that while I'm up there you three had better get your plans worked out in detail, in readiness for any move which the *Windward* may make. We don't want to improvise ; it's risky."

"Very good, officer of the watch," replied Dick, somewhat jestingly. "Mind you don't catch a cold up there ; and if you go to sleep, make sure you snore loudly, so that we can come and take over from you ! "

For his reply he received a meaningful look ; and then Chris went out through the awning, and took up her post on the stern of the yacht.

Down below, the three male members of the crew began another spell of discussion and planning. It was finally agreed that if the *Windward* did come past them into the New Cut, then John and Dick would follow in the dinghy, and see if they could get more definite evidence of the activities of the mysterious yacht and its crew. They would muffle the rowlocks as best they could, and would also take a fishing-rod so that they would have some excuse if they were seen.

Dick went out to the dinghy with some old pieces of rag, in order to do the muffling, while John turned on his radio in an attempt to try to catch any further message which might be sent out, and also to listen out for Hugh's possible call at 10 p.m.

For some time there was no activity on either the short-wave band used by *Windward*, or the Hilversum wavelength on which Hugh had planned to oscillate. While he was turning the controls and waiting, John found himself asking Mr. Vincent a question.

Mr. Vincent was a strangely-attractive character to John ; he seemed so calm, so sure of things, and withal so understanding ; the sort of man in whom it would be easy to confide ; he so obviously held the complete confidence of his own children that there was no possibility of his misunderstanding or taking advantage of his new friend.

" Mr. Vincent ; I couldn't help noticing the three of you when I came in just now. You were praying. Do you really believe that there is anything in it ? Our Science Master at school drummed it into us that the Universe was worked on fixed principles, and by fixed laws, and that it is silly to expect them to be upset merely to suit the wishes of a few unimportant mortals."

Mr. Vincent looked encouragingly at John as if he were waiting for him to continue. "Yes," he said, sympathetically; "I suppose it is a bit of a problem."

Rather thankful that he had not been snubbed straightway, John continued. "Well, you see, I was thinking about the vast size of the universe; looking at all those stars just now; it seems hard to believe that the One Who made them (if He did) is interested in people like us."

Mr. Vincent paused a moment, then replied, "That's a further point, John; I do not think that the question of size or space has much to do with it. After all, you don't consider a big man to be more important than a little man; nor do you consider that a piece of rock is more valuable than a piece of gold simply because it is a thousand times bigger. Not only that, when you look into the very smallest parts of Nature, you see that they are made with perfect and beautiful detail; in fact, there is a sense in which some of the smallest things are more wonderful than, for example, a massive mountain range. I think it is plain enough that what matters is quality, not quantity. An elephant is much bigger than a man, but it is obviously a good deal lower in the scale of creation."

"Yes," replied John, thoughtfully, "I suppose you are right there; it is rather a stupid

argument, but it does not answer my first difficulty about the 'laws' of Nature, and the
universe."

"No, but there is an answer, I think. Surely
it is possible for the laws themselves to be under
the control of higher powers. There is the law
of gravity, for instance. If I let a book go, it
will fall to the ground ; but if you catch it half-
way, you have interfered with that law, and you
have controlled it by your own superior power.
You may even *lift* the book, which is a direct
reversal of the law of gravity. If you think back
you will realize that when the book is lifted, it is
not merely because the muscles of your arm have
obeyed certain laws, or rules of Nature. Your
arm and its muscles are obeying the commands of
something else."

"You mean my *mind*," interrupted John.

"Yes," said Mr. Vincent ; " and your mind
is able to act in many different ways without
obeying any 'law of Nature', as you call it.
If your mind can do that, and if it is true (and
it seems perfectly reasonable to me) that the
universe was made by God, Who is a Person,
able to think and to choose, why should *He* not
interfere, and cause things to happen in an
unexpected way ? I believe He often does it,
but if you want some specially clear examples,
you have them in the stories of what happened
when the Lord Jesus was on earth. John tells
us in his Gospel about God's Son, Who had

been God's Agent in creating the world ; when He came to earth, He did just what I've been talking about. He healed diseases, He calmed storms, He even raised the dead. It was the sort of thing you would expect from Someone Who could make Nature His servant, and knew it thoroughly."

"Yes, I suppose there is something in what you say," said John, still somewhat dubious.

"You take your radio, for instance," went on Mr. Vincent. "Supposing you were to bring into this cabin some ignorant native from the tropical jungle, who had never seen such a thing as a radio set before. Supposing you were to say to him, 'I am going to produce voices, music, and other sounds in many different languages, out of that box ; and some of those voices are going to come from hundreds of miles away.' The native would reply, 'It is impossible.' He would say no man could make his voice heard more than a couple of miles away, and most certainly you cannot get a lot of musicians in that box !' "

"I think I can see what's coming," said John.

"Yes, it is fairly obvious. You would then go to your radio set, turn on the current, and produce the music. The native might refuse to be convinced at first, just as there are some people who do not believe in prayer, in spite of the evidence ; but in the end he would have to admit you were right. What would have made

your 'miracle' possible ?    Simply your superior
knowledge of the laws of the universe, and your
ability to use them for your own purposes.    If
God is the Creator of all, He therefore under-
stands them perfectly—far, far better than any
man.    Why should He not then produce results
which seem incredible to us ?    They are simply
the result of His own perfect knowledge of the
world which He has made."

The conversation was interrupted suddenly by
the return of Dick, who had muffled the rowlocks,
and had prepared the dinghy for its possible
adventure.

"Hullo, Dick !" said Mr. Vincent.  "Everything in order out there ?    John and I have been
having a little discussion on the subject of prayer,
and the possibility of its being answered.    I've
been trying to explain the theory of it all."

"Wouldn't you do even better if you spoke
about the *facts* that *you* have seen, Dad ? " said
Dick, respectfully.    "Theories can always be
questioned and argued over, but some of the
things that have happened to you cannot be
explained away.    There was that miraculous
supply of food, which arrived when you were
eating what you thought would be your last
meal, when the bandits had cut you off from all
outside supply ; there was the discovery of water
during that long trek across the Mongolian desert,
when you were pioneering ; there was the sudden
cure of your companion, when the nearest doctor

was hundreds of miles away, and when you had tried every treatment you knew, without success ; there was the time when the cholera raged in the town, and you went in and out among the people, risking infection all day long, day after day, and yet you were kept free from it. You can account for one odd happening like that, here and there, by calling it coincidence ; but you can't explain all your experiences like that. That's fact, not theory."

" Perhaps you're right, Dick ; but I feel that we should be able to give John here a satisfactory explanation of how it all happens ; these scientific young men of today demand to be shown not only what happens, but *how* it happens.   And I think they're quite right ; provided they consider *all* the evidence, we have nothing to fear.   If Christianity's true, it will stand all the examinations that people like to submit it to ; we've nothing to hide ! "

" Thank you very much, Mr. Vincent," said John.   " I can't say that I've really given the matter much honest thought.   I've just taken for granted what people have said ; especially such people as our science master.   I suppose I've really been doing what I have often accused the Christians of doing ; taking things for granted, and refusing to think them through for myself."

" It's more than likely ; that's the pity of it. People are apt to forget that some of the so-called ' scientists,' who claim to look at everything with completely open minds, are actually as biased and as narrow-minded along their own line as, say, a politician may be along his. As a matter of fact, I think that. . . ."

Suddenly John interrupted. Glancing at his wrist-watch, he said, " It is just on ten o'clock ; it's time we listened to see if Hugh has any message for us."

He turned the dial of the set, and as he tuned in on Hilversum, he looked up excitedly.

" There he is," he cried. " Hear him whistling ? "

Sure enough, there was the up and down note of oscillation ; then it stopped for a moment. (" A signal coming," remarked John.)

After a slight pause, they heard the unmistakable dots and dashes of a morse signal. They were rather rough, as would be expected from someone trying to employ the oscillation of an ordinary radio set for that purpose. However, it was clear enough to be understood, and John noted down the message. The others looked eagerly over his shoulder at what he was writing. They read :

RING ME P.H. 4315 AT ONCE. HANGING ON.  HUGH.

" I wonder what Hugh wants to speak to you about," said Mr. Vincent. " It must be something important, or he would not have sent that message by morse ; the only way to ring him is to take the dinghy and row across to Horsey staithe. I will check it on the map, but I think I noticed a 'phone box marked there when I looked it up earlier on."

He quickly opened up the chart of the Broads, and found it to be as he had said.

" What happens if the *Windward* comes past while I'm away ? " asked John.

" He'll hardly have time to sail up the New Cut and back again before you return," said Dick. " What I suggest is that we both go in the dinghy, and then we can row all out and relieve one another half-way. The sooner we get going the better, as Hugh is waiting for us."

## Chapter 12

### HUGH MAKES A 'PHONE CALL

JOHN and Dick collected a stock of sixpences and pennies, in order to be quite sure of getting the 'phone call successfully, and were very soon slipping across the now smooth waters of the Mere towards the public staithe in the north-east corner. First John, and then Dick, bent to the oars with all the power they could command, and they moved speedily along. There was a new moon, shedding a little light, reflected on the wavelets, and making their task easier. The wind had dropped considerably, but the sky was not completely clear, and the thin, rapidly moving wisps of high cloud gave promise of plenty of wind in store. After about a quarter of an hour they found themselves approaching the timber landing-stage, which was quite deserted ; they tied the dinghy securely, and set off at a steady trot along the narrow lane which led in the direction of the village. Some five minutes of this brought them to the cluster of cottages which made up the centre of Horsey village.

There were a few lights shining out over the roadway, especially from the local public house, where the landlord was busy clearing up after his last customers had gone. In one corner of the open gravel yard in front of this building they saw the telephone box, with its own light gleaming cheerfully.

John went quickly in, placed his money on the box, in readiness, and set about getting his number. He had no trouble, and was soon listening to Hugh's familiar voice.

" Sorry to fetch you out at this time of night," said Hugh. " I've got some first-rate news for you. Are you all right ? "

" Yes ; everything's going smoothly ; you needn't apologize ; Dick and I just love these rowing expeditions in the light of the moon. Come on, what's the news ?  It had better be hot ! "

" I think I've got a line on that code."

" Whaaaat ! !   How d'you manage that ? Whose brainwave ? "

" It's a long story ; I can't tell you everything now.  I overheard a conversation in the Stores here, when I came in to get some matches. I'm not absolutely sure, mind, and a lot depends on what newspapers you've got on board the *Sabrina*."

" You sound even more off-the-line than ever ! "

" No, seriously ; you remember that card we found, with ' D.T.' and then some numbers on it ? "

" Yes ; we've been puzzling over it again tonight."

" Well, suppose ' D.T.' stands for ' *Daily*

*Telegraph,*' and the numbers stand for dates ; i.e., 7/9 stands for the edition of the 7th of September. Then suppose the four-figure numbers of the messages we heard stand for Page number, Column number, Line number and Word number, respectively. Each four-figure number would give you one word. You could make up almost any message from one issue of a paper like that. And unless the people who were after you had exactly the same issue, they would never get the message ! "

" My word ! Perhaps you're right ! How on earth did you think all that out ? Pure genius, without a doubt ! "

" No ; it was a combination of luck and memory ; I'll explain it all later ; in any case, it's not absolutely certain."

" No, and I'm not so sure about that word ' luck,' either ; but that's something else we'll have to discuss another time."

John went on to explain the position on the Mere, and the plans they had in mind for the night.

" I hope the excitement won't be all over when you catch up with me," said Hugh, rather enviously, when he had heard the full plan. " Mind you don't get turned into mincemeat or something ! "

" We'll try to save some fun for you," replied John. " We must get back now, so I'll ring off. You had better stand by your radio at four o'clock tomorrow morning, as well as at six, just to make sure ; we may have something urgent to tell you."

" Right you are ; I'll be listening.  All the best ; good night ! "

" Good night ! "

John rang off, and quickly outlined the news to Dick.  He felt convinced that Hugh had found the clue.  " Can you remember the dates on that code card you found ? " he asked.  " We might make sure of getting a paper by asking in the village here ; at this place, for instance."

Dick thought a moment.

" I ought to be able to remember ; yes, I've got it !  The first line was, ' 1/10—10/10 15/9 : ' I suppose that means that from the 1st to the 10th of October (that's now) they are using the *Daily Telegraph* issued on the 15th September."

" Yes, but if they're signalling to Diamatia, how can their friends there get hold of an English newspaper ? "

" That's easy ; English papers are flown over daily, and are sold in all the European countries. Besides, there's always the diplomatic bag. There would be no difficulty about that."

" Our job, then, is to make sure of getting a *Daily Telegraph* for September 15th ; we may have one on the boat, but I'm very doubtful ; we used some newspapers for packing our things, and it might be among them.  It would be better to make sure of one here.  Let's try the innkeeper."

Dick walked across to the doorway, from which a light shone, and gave a firm knock.

A surprised-looking publican answered. No, he didn't take the *Daily Telegraph*. The only place he knew where one might be found was the vicarage, just along the road.

Dick and John thanked him, and ran in the direction he had given.

They saw that there was a light still burning in several of the downstairs rooms, and so they took their courage in both hands and knocked at the front door. The Vicar, a friendly-looking, youngish man, answered their knock ; he also looked somewhat startled. The request they made did not lessen his surprise. They gave no definite reason, but simply stated that it was a matter of personal importance to them. Being used to the strange ways of Broads holiday-makers, the Vicar said no more, but rummaged around in a cupboard under the stairs, and very soon produced what they wanted. They thanked him warmly, and set off again to the dinghy, in high spirits.

Within a quarter of an hour they were manœuvring the dinghy towards *Sabrina*, and Chris, who was still keeping her watch, reached for the painter and pulled them alongside.

" I'll take over the watch," suggested Dick. " You go down below and hear the news, Chris. Besides, they'll need your brilliant deductive powers for the working-out of those messages ! "

" Thanks a lot ; for the first part of your speech, at any rate."

Soon Chris, John, and Mr. Vincent were busy working on the code messages which Dick had written down when listening to the mysterious transmitter the previous day.

John had recorded only snatches of the first two messages he had heard, but he had taken down the third one, which had been transmitted during the first part of the ill-fated race on Horsey, in full.

" I've just remembered," he said, as he was looking for the paper on which he had written, " we saw the captain of the *Windward* reading from an old copy of the *Daily Telegraph* as we entered Horsey Mere. It certainly seems to fit in ! "

They set to work on the complete message. Each four-figure number led them to a word or numeral as they turned, first to the page, then the column, then the line, and finally the word indicated. The message took shape.

> " Hope to collect the three tonight. Leaving depôt six Tuesday. Meeting as arranged. Yellow."

" That settles it ! " cried John, triumphantly. " ' The three ' must be the escaped prisoners ; the ' depôt ' is the place where they have arranged to pick them up, I suppose. What does ' Yellow ' stand for ? "

" As it comes at the end, I expect it's some sort

of signature " volunteered Chris. " I've got it !
' Yellow '—' Craven '—craven means cowardly ;
yellow's the colour ! "

" My word, what a brainwave ! " broke in
Mr. Vincent. " I really think we ought to
inform the police now ; we have enough evidence,
surely."

" Can't we leave it a little longer, Dad ? "
pleaded Chris. " After all, we've more or less
got them cornered. They must leave by way of
Potter Heigham and Yarmouth, and we can have
them stopped at either place. They have no
cause for suspecting us, now. Let them collect
these other chaps ; if they're interrupted, they
may not go for them. Besides, if we go to the
local constable, he'll think we're ragging him."

" Very well, then ; but we must take care ;
these are obviously dangerous men. We can't
afford to run unnecessary risks. We will certainly notify the police tomorrow."

" You must also remember, Mr. Vincent,
that we haven't absolutely pinned this matter on
to the *Windward* for certain. We heard signals
on one occasion when it seemed that she was
not transmitting. We had to assume that there
was also a transmitter in a house fairly close by.
It may have been that one all the time. I
know the coincidences are strong, but it is not
certain. If they get up to any tricks tonight,
we can be quite sure of our case."

" The light's gone out," called Dick, from the

stern. "But there's no sign of a move. I can just see the tip of their mast against the skyline."

"And it's time our lights went out," said Mr. Vincent. "It's half-past eleven, and we should be asleep by now; we may have excitement to-morrow. Those of us who are carrying on the watch will need every bit of sleep we can get. I suggest that John relieves Dick at 2 a.m. and I'll relieve John at 4. You must be sure to give me a good shake, as I am sleeping very deeply these days."

"Suits me," called down Dick's voice from outside the awning.

John was about to throw himself, without undressing, on the bunk along one side of the cabin, when he noticed Chris looking expectantly at Mr. Vincent. The latter reached along the shelf which ran the length of the cabin, just beneath the portholes, and produced a small volume. John recognized it as a New Testament.

"We usually have prayers together before we turn in," said Mr. Vincent. "I hope you will join us tonight?"

"Certainly," replied John, rather glad of the opportunity of seeing this side of his new friends at such close quarters.

Mr. Vincent opened at a place which was apparently marked, and began to read. It was not in the familiar words of the ordinary Bible; John guessed it was some modern translation.

It made the passage (from one of Paul's epistles) seem as if it was written directly to people like himself. The language was up-to-date and fresh. And Mr. Vincent read it with such obvious warmth of conviction, although without any trace of dramatics, that John wondered at the living force and up-to-dateness of the words he heard.

> " God has chosen the things which the world regards as foolish, in order to put its wise men to shame . . . to prevent any mortal man from boasting in the presence of God. . . ."

Then Mr. Vincent prayed. As he prayed, speaking in simple language as one very familiar with the way of prayer, who had learned to rely completely upon the wisdom and power o God, John felt that here was a man who had learned lessons such as the " wise " men of the world scarcely even dreamed about. There was no denying the simple faith which Mr. Vincent had towards God, nor could there be any question as to the reality of God to him.

This was a new experience for John. He had heard plenty of prayers recited in a formal sort of way; it was not long since he himself had repeated a set of requests just before he went to sleep each night ; but this living fellowship, this simple confidence, this sense of the nearness and reality of God—this was different. It was even desirable, he thought ; something needed to make life complete. He wondered how he had missed this side of Christianity for so long. He was learning fast.

Chris added a simple word of prayer, with a special reference to Hugh at Potter Heigham, and then they turned in.

Chris had lit the primus before coming into the cabin, and so they were able to enjoy a cup of hot cocoa and some biscuits and cheese before they went to sleep.

Outside, Dick began his vigil.

## Chapter 13

### WINDWARD TAKES ON PASSENGERS

THE next thing John knew was that he was being shaken vigorously, and that Dick was whispering loudly in his ear:

" Come on, rouse up ! They're on the move ! John ! John ! It's me, Dick ! The *Windward*'s moving this way."

John came slowly to himself, for he had by now settled into a heavy sleep.

" All right : I'll be up in a moment. Don't you think we ought to tell your father ? We don't want him to wake up and miss us."

" No ; he needs a good sleep. I'll tell Chris ; she can give him the message : we'll almost certainly have to follow *Windward* up the New Cut."

" Yes ; and it's just struck me that she will probably come back again before dawn, so that she can be in her mooring-place on the other side of Horsey when daylight comes ; otherwise it would look too suspicious."

" Right ! Just a moment, then ; I'll go and see Chris."

Dick passed into the fore cabin, and, after waking Chris with some difficulty, he told her the news. " We'll follow up in the dinghy," he said. " One or other of us will report back here before four o'clock ; if we don't see anything interesting, we'll both come back by then. If you don't hear from one or both of us by that time, warn Hugh at Potter Heigham ; we've arranged for him to listen out at four. The transmitter needs only to be switched on. You can use the microphone to speak to him. You had better warn the police as well."

"All right. Take care. There's no need to run risks ! "

"We won't ; at least, not too many ! See you soon."

Dick and John made their way out on to the deck. The night was clear, but the new moon was already waning, so that soon only the star-light would break the absolute darkness. The wind had risen again, and was blowing quite strongly from the south. It was cool, but not uncomfortably cold.

John peered out across the black surface of the Mere ; after a while, his eyes grew accustomed to the dark and he could see a black shape moving slowly towards them, coming in a direct line across towards the mouth of the New Cut. It showed no lights, and looked almost ghostlike as it slid silently through the water. There was no doubt that it intended to come right past *Sabrina*'s mooring.

"We must lie low as she passes," said John. "I suggest we get round behind the awning."

" Good idea ! "

They moved round to the hidden side of the yacht, and waited, their nerves tense, as the sense of an overshadowing menace seemed to brood over them in the still, dark night. The rustle of wind through the reeds, the occasional hoot of an owl, the soft splash of a nearby water-rat—these were the only sounds to be heard. *Windward* was out of sight now that they were behind the awning and no longer commanded a clear view across the Mere ; they could only wait, keyed up and wondering.

Suddenly a large, dark shadow almost filled the narrow entrance to the New Cut. Dick and John stiffened. Slowly, mysteriously, the *Windward* moved up towards them ; as her mainsail eased out, the ropes ran quietly through blocks which had obviously been well oiled.

She moved steadily past, a dark silhouette sitting stiffly at the helm ; she might have been bearing a cargo of the dead, with a spectre at the tiller. There was an air of evil about her, heightened by the darkness all around.

The steersman's head turned slowly as she passed *Sabrina* ; whoever he was, he took a long look at her. He gave no sign of having seen the two watchers. *Windward* continued on her way, more slowly than ever, the wind being blanketed by a clump of bushes.

When she had passed round the first bend, Dick and John, armed with a couple of torches and some chocolate, climbed into the dinghy, and pushed off.

"It's quieter to use the oar as a quant pole," suggested Dick. "Sound carries a long way over water."

He set to work, John taking the tiny rudder with which the dinghy was provided for use when its small sail was hoisted. They kept close in to the bank, slowed down as they reached the bend, and looked carefully ahead before they continued on the next stretch of water.

This was quite a long straight section, which made it difficult to keep out of sight. By dint of keeping well under the lee of the bank, they managed it, however, and kept the *Windward*, whose sail stood out in black relief against the sky, well within their vision.

"This Cut is very narrow," whispered John. "We don't want to get caught when the *Windward* returns ; we had better keep our eyes open for a dyke, leading off the main stream, in which we can lie up. She may not spend long here ; I imagine she will turn straight round when she has picked up her passengers."

"You're right ! You know, I've a feeling she's going to moor up by that windmill there."

"Looks a likely place ; it's a disused one, isn't it ? "

"I'm not sure ; but if it were, it would make an ideal hide-out if anyone wanted to hang up for a few days out of the public eye ! "

The windmill in question could be seen about three hundred yards ahead ; it was just a dark, almost shapeless outline, set against the starlit sky.

They drew closer to the *Windward* as she moved smoothly along ; then her shadow grew suddenly larger.

" She's turning across the stream," said John. " Just by the mill, too ! "

" Let's moor the dinghy in this dyke here on the port side ; perhaps we can walk along the bank."

" Suits me.  Hold tight ! "

Dick swung the nose of the dinghy into a narrow channel which branched off the main stream ; it was heavily overgrown with reeds. They slid gently into these, bumping softly on the muddy bottom.  It was an ideal spot for concealment.  They tied the painter to a clump of reeds, and jumped ashore.

" If we walk along the lower edge of the bank, we can't be seen from the mill," suggested John.

Here the fenland was, as so often in that part of the country, well below the level of the main stream.  The windmills had been used in former times for pumping the water up from the low-lying fields into the dykes and broads, which were part of the giant drainage-system.

John and Dick made their way carefully and silently towards the mill.  They could see the sail of the *Windward* as she swung round, head to wind, preparatory to mooring up. Then her sails were allowed to run free, and she came to a standstill close by the mill.

The two watchers were by now quite close, picking their way carefully over the marshy ground at the base of the river bank. Finally they came to a fence some ten yards from the mill. They could not cross it without coming into the open, so they stayed where they were, taking cover by lying down flat in the tall grass and reeds.

There was no sign of life in the mill itself. Its sails were not badly destroyed, though the majority of the small slats had been broken. They revolved slowly in the wind, creaking as they did so. The sound they made, coupled with the general loneliness and desolation of the immediate neighbourhood, and the ominous black shadow of the *Windward*, sent a tingling down the spines of the two watchers as they lay in the damp grass.

They saw *Windward* tie up, close to the mill. Then the figure of a man, who, they thought, was Captain Craven, was seen to jump ashore. He went up to the mill, took a quick look round, and then disappeared through the half-ruined doorway. This was on the side of the mill where Dick and John were, and they saw his torch flash on as he entered. Two short flashes followed by two long ones. ("The same as their radio call-sign," whispered John.) Then they heard him

call out, in a subdued, hoarse, penetrating voice :
" Vallin, Simonov, Klansen ; we have come !
This is Craven—I've got the boat ready. Come
down ! Hurry ! We must get moving quickly."

Until that moment there had been no sign
that the mill was occupied. Then Dick and
John heard three successive thuds ; three heavy
men had apparently dropped from a height to
the floor of the mill. The watchers in the grass
saw the light of the torch moving round ; evidently Captain Craven was examining the new
arrivals one by one. Then a heavily-accented
voice could be clearly heard :

" We are so glad to see you, Captain Craven.
We had great difficulty in getting here ; we have
had no food since two days. This was a good
hiding-place, however ; nobody has been near
us. What do we do now ? "

John and Dick strained to hear the answer.

" We sail for the Fatherland at once. I must
get back to Horsey Mere before dawn ; two
foolish young Englishmen seem to have become
suspicious of me. I've dealt with them, I think ;
but we must not run any risks. We simply must
not draw any attention to ourselves. Come
aboard right away ; don't show any kind of light."

Three men, each carrying a bundle, came out
of the mill, followed by Captain Craven. They
began to move across to the *Windward* silently,
in single file.

Suddenly Craven stopped.

9

"You three go on board," he said. "Introduce yourselves to the 'First Mate,' Gregor Yakolev, alias George Roberts. You'll have heard of him. I think you have met him before. He's a patriotic Britisher!"

This last sentence was spoken in tones of contempt; it was greeted with low chuckles. Apparently Captain Craven had tickled their sense of humour. He continued:

"I'd like to have a look at that fence; if it is anything like new, I could do with a length of wire for a small repair job on the yacht."

To their horror, Dick and John realized that this sudden decision of his would bring him near to where they lay. There was nothing they could do about it, for if they moved they would give their presence away. They could only lie still and hope to remain unobserved.

Captain Craven came across in their direction, shone his torch on the wire, felt it, and then walked back to the yacht.

"Shall we run for it?" whispered John.

"If we do, he's sure to spot us. He seems to have given up the idea of getting that wire."

Dick's prophecy proved disastrously wrong. A few moments later Captain Craven reappeared, together with another man, and came back to the fence. He held what appeared to be some sort of tool in his hand.

"I caught one of the shrouds on an overhanging concrete bank, yesterday," he was saying.

"I think it would be wise to reinforce it somewhat, and this wire looks just the thing. The farmer will not begrudge it in a good cause ; and it's almost brand new."

He came up close to where Dick and John lay hidden.

"You hold this end, after I've cut it," he said to his companion. "Then I'll cut the other end, and you can coil it up. This should give us six yards of useful wire."

He quickly cut the length he had named, and was waiting for his companion to coil it up, when Dick, affected by the damp cold of his position, burst out with a sudden sneeze. He had hardly had time to think of suppressing it, even if he could have done so.

"What the . . .?" exclaimed Captain Craven's companion.

"Run for it, John ! " shouted Dick.

"Get them ! " yelled Captain Craven, jumping on John, who was struggling to his feet.

Dick did manage to pick himself up, and began to run, but the other man was powerfully built, and could move with surprising speed. Stumbling as he crossed a particularly marshy section, he felt himself pushed violently in the back, and he fell heavily on his face ; his pursuer jumped on his back, and winded him as a result. He felt himself half-dragged, half-carried to where Captain Craven was still sitting on Dick, pinning him to the ground.

" Take your prisoner to the yacht," he ordered.
" Then send one of the others to help me with
this one ; I daren't move from here, as I'm not
too sure of holding him on my own."

" Very good, sir ! "

Dick could feel from the force of the grip in
which he was held that there was little chance
of escape. He did try to trip his captor up, as
they moved towards the boat, but he only suffered
the more as a result, and so decided to go quietly.
Submission seemed to be the best policy for the
time being. The other men had come out into
the well on hearing the commotion, and they
helped Dick's captor embark his prisoner. One
of them went to the help of Captain Craven.
Soon John joined Dick in the *Windward's* cabin,
a fierce-looking guard on either side.

Captain Craven held a short whispered conference in the well with one of the three men who
had come from the mill. Then he came in and
faced the two intruders. The others grouped
themselves around him, their hard, cruel faces
made almost grotesque by the flickering of the
dim oil-lamp with which the cabin was lighted.

" Aha ! My friend from the *Viking*, eh ?
How very interesting ! so you're not safely moored
up at Potter Heigham, after all ? "

" Doesn't look like it ! " replied John.

" What a pity !—for all of us, I mean." The
voice was still quiet, refined, almost silken in its
smoothness. " And how did you come to be

lying in the grass near the old mill, eh ? ''

" We're fond of sleeping out ; very healthy custom, you know," suggested John.

The voice hardened.

" This is no joke, you young fool ! So far as I am concerned your friend and yourself are just a couple of stupid nuisances. But you have put your hands in a very hot place ; it may be that you will get burned, see ? We can't afford to be kind to you ; too much is at stake. This is just an adventure to you ; to us it is a matter of life or death. What were you doing ? Out with it ! How did you follow us ? ''

" We're not telling you anything—that's flat," replied John. " The sooner you let us go, the better for everyone ; you don't want a couple of innocent Englishmen on your hands."

" Silence, you, if you've nothing better to say ! I'll ask for your advice when I feel I have need of it. You two know too much ; we can't let you loose now ; in fact, we shall have to keep you for some time to come. I'm afraid you are going to suffer a little inconvenience ; it can't be helped ; you must console yourselves with the thought that it might be a great deal worse."

Craven paused, thinking for a moment or two. Then he gave his orders—crisp and clear.

" Vallin, you must be responsible for these two interfering fools. Tie them up securely, and put them in the forepeak ; then stand guard over them until further orders. You must gag them well, so that they cannot make any noise when we pass their boat."

" Verry good, Captain Craven," came the reply, in heavily-accented English. " But would it not be better to dump them overboard in the water right away ?  Let them drown, and be finished with them."

" No point in it ; their friends must know enough about us by now to stop us ever coming here again.  All that we can hope for is to get away from here tonight, and out to sea before the alarm is raised.  We might just do it ; we must hurry.  But there's no need to have unnecessary crimes on our hands.  They'll make useful ballast if the North Sea is rough ! "

Craven then disappeared outside, and soon *Windward* was moving again.  Meanwhile the man called Vallin was busy, with the help of his two companions, trussing John and Dick very thoroughly, and gagging them tightly.  From the looks he gave them, they gathered that they would have little mercy at his hands.  They wondered how far he would allow them to be taken before he had his own ruthless way.

John was thinking hard ; he did not see how the *Windward* could possibly get through Yarmouth before daybreak ; the wind was not too favourable, and there were only about five more hours of darkness left.  By dawn, the alarm would have been given, and *Windward's* way of escape closed.  When they had been thoroughly tied

up, Vallin called Captain Craven, in order that
he might check them over.

" Don't bother to put them in the forepeak,"
he said, surveying them. " They can't come to
any harm down here ; let them stay put."

John and Dick signalled " Thanks very much "
with their eyes, for although they were far from
comfortable, they were much better off than they
would have been in the confined space of the
forepeak.

" We'll soon be passing *Sabrina*," thought
Dick. " Chris would get a shock if she knew
how near I was to her now ! And how far I may
be in a few hours' time ! Pity I can't let her
know ! "

Just then, Captain Craven came down into
the cabin again. Giving Dick a push, he rolled
him over so that his eyes were opposite a porthole.
He then motioned to Dick to look outside. Dick
stared into the darkness. As his eyes grew
accustomed to the gloom, he saw the faint outline of *Sabrina* slipping past ; she lay dark and
still ; Mr. Vincent and Chris were apparently
enjoying deep slumber.

" I'm so sorry, my young intruders," said
Captain Craven, shortly after. " It had to be ;
you should have kept your noses out of our
business. Whether or not you see your friends
again depends upon a number of different
things. We shall have to see. I think I may
order your gags to be removed shortly."

He then went back to the well. *Windward* was now scudding across the open waters of Horsey Mere. She heeled gently in the soft night breeze ; so long as it remained as quiet as that, there was every hope that Dick and John would be rescued. They had both worked things out in a similar way, knowing that the alarm would be raised, and were not feeling too depressed.

It was then that they received their next—and most unpleasant—shock. There was a whirring sound, followed by a steady vibration. Dick could just hear the murmur of what must have been a very efficient exhaust-silencing system. The vibration increased, and it was obvious that *Windward's* speed was rising, since they could hear the slap, slap, of the water against her hull becoming more and more violent. They were obviously moving much faster.

Dick caught John's eye. They exchanged a look of surprise and dismay. This was something for which they had not allowed. *Windward* apparently had a powerful auxiliary motor. With the favourable tide which would then be running she might easily make Yarmouth before day-light, and so be away out to sea before the authorities had been warned.

Captain Craven re-entered the cabin. A look of satisfaction appeared on his face. He began to speak again :

" A little surprise, eh ? She is a very efficient craft, this *Windward*. If you had not spoiled my plans completely, she would have been very useful to me during the next few months. Now I shall have to scrap her and start all over again, if that is possible."

His look grew more fierce ; his voice took on a higher, somewhat strained, pitch, as of a man who suffered from a blinding obsession. He continued, more excitedly :

" You owe me a very great debt, my unknown friends ! I don't know how you came to stumble into our scheme, but I would have you know that you have spoiled some very careful plans ; and you have caused me to waste a great deal of money. You deserve to meet a very un-pleasant end—with the herrings on the Dogger Bank, shall we say ? You stupid boys ! (His voice grew harsher, and rose higher.) You shall not thwart me ! I will succeed, for the sake of the Fatherland ! I have come to detest England. Now I play my part in the service of Diamatia, the only nation which can save civilization ! England—she is finished ! Cinemas, jazz, vulgar comedians, and food supplies—that is all that the ' noble ' Englishman thinks of. No spiritual force ! No great ideal ! Just a nation of de-cadent food-and-pleasure-seekers. Bah ! It's time she was wound up and a new progressive order established ! "

Dick and John listened in astonishment ; this gave them at least some understanding of the mind of the man into whose hands they had fallen. It was hardly a comforting insight. John was particularly thoughtful, for he could see quite plainly that his life had a good deal in it which fitted Captain Craven's scathing attack on England in general. He had hardly awoken to the fact that there might be something more in this business of living than just having as good a time as possible, gathering as much material comfort as possible, and living a reasonably respectable life. He found himself asking a question which he could not answer : What really was *his own* positive aim in life ? He had gone on trying for various targets, for a number of reasons ; sometimes because his parents had wanted him to ; sometimes because other people thought better of him for doing so ; sometimes because of the sensation of pleasure which he himself enjoyed when he achieved anything. But there was no single dominating aim ; no great life-purpose which could really satisfy and employ his fullest powers. It was a strange moment for a young man to discover that there was a vacuum at the very centre of his life, but that was the discovery he made then. He was recalled to face the ugly present, however, by the continuation of Captain Craven's speech spoken in a softer, lower tone.

" I think you can do without those gags now ; you can guess what we are doing. We are just coming out of Horsey Mere ; we shall be at Potter Heigham in half an hour, at Acle in another hour, and out at sea by dawn ! The tide is flowing very helpfully. By the time your friends wake up, you'll maybe be tasting the joys of dinghy-sailing in the North Sea. Vallin, remove those gags. If either of them starts making a noise or fuss, silence him with the butt end of your revolver."

He handed over the said weapon, and Vallin undid the bandages. Dick and John began to breathe freely again. Captain Craven gave them one more word of instruction :

" You may talk softly ; but no more than that. When we go through Potter Heigham and Acle, you will keep perfectly quiet. Understand ? "

" Very good," replied Dick, " but we're not making any promises."

" I don't expect you to ; but if you're wise, you'll respect the butt end of that revolver. If you do attempt to make a noise, not only will Vallin hurt you, but I shall see that the gags remain on you for the rest of the trip ! "

" Right you are ; we understand. Thanks for taking them off now."

## Chapter 14

### AN UNUSUAL DISCUSSION

CAPTAIN CRAVEN disappeared again, and soon John and Hugh could tell by the changing motion of the *Windward* that they were moving through the narrow, winding waters of Meadow Dyke.

" Pretty bad fix, Dick. I'm sorry I landed you in this mess."

" That's all right, John ; I'm enjoying it in a way. I must say that the noise of that engine gave me a shock, though. However, I've been reminding myself of a verse from the Bible which Father used often to quote in his letters when things looked black : ' All things work together for good to them that love God.' He used to call that—' The Divine Conspiracy ' ; because, he said, very few people recognized what God was doing ; even those who knew Him were often unable to understand or even discover His purpose. But it's true. Hope isn't gone yet, John."

He put as much meaning into the words of that last sentence as he possibly could, for he dared not speak openly about what either Chris or Hugh might do as a result of the planned 4 a.m. radio contact. Vallin was watching them remorselessly ; he would certainly not miss the force of any clues which they might drop.

"I say, Dick."

"Yes, old chap?"

"There's one good thing about our having met."

"What's that?"

"You've given me a new idea of what this business of 'being a Christian' means. You and your sister and your father, that is."

"I'm glad to hear you say that; didn't you know before?"

"I thought I did; I've discovered I didn't. My first shake-up came while I was away with the family, at a little Cornish seaside town, in August. There was a group of fellows there who were running some meetings on the sands, for kids. I wasn't very interested, but one of them got talking to me one day, and invited me round to the house where they were all staying. I had supper with them, and also had a good long yarn with them afterwards. Several of them were Varsity men, ex-Service types who had seen plenty of life. They were a mixed crowd. I thought some of the girls looked rather attractive, in contrast to the average seaside-resort specimens. They didn't go in for make-up and so on, and I thought they were a good deal more frank and pleasant than the usual brand."

"What did you talk about? I've several friends who do that sort of work in the summer. I should like to hear."

"I was coming to that. It wasn't so much

what they said that impressed me. Though I must say they gave some of my stock ' Objections to Christianity ' a very rough handling. They made me look like the out-of-date believer in second-hand ideas that I had always imagined Christians to be ! But there was something over and above that. It's hard to describe."

" Carry on," said Dick, encouragingly ; " I think I have an idea what you mean."

" It was their bearing ; their . . . er . . . attitude to life as a whole. They had a purpose ; they knew what they were here for. They had standards far higher than I would have imagined ; I mean standards of right and wrong, truth, honesty, sincerity and so on. But it was that sense of purpose which impressed me. In spite of all that some of them had seen—in fact, because of it, in some cases—they could look out on the world and make some sort of sense of it ; and they had a crystal-clear objective. They had to get the message of God across to other people at all costs. They believed that it was true, they practised it themselves, and they tried all they could to pass it on to others. What is more, they found it all very satisfying. It shook me ; I've been wondering ever since. It wasn't just emotion ; they had good reason for what they believed. And now you and Chris and your father come along, also sharing the same certainty, and enjoying the same peace of mind. What Captain Craven was

saying about England today was also a pretty
accurate description of a fellow I know, named
John Wilson. It's perfectly true—I haven't
really got a worth-while purpose ; and there are
thousands more like me. We can see fairly
clearly what is wrong with the world ; but we
haven't the foggiest idea of what to do about it.
We find, in fact, that the things which trouble
the world at large—envy, mistrust, jealousy,
hatred and so on—are present in our own natures;
some are worse than others, but so long as we
are infected with these poisonous things, who are
we to start putting others right ?   Tell me some
more !  I suppose it was easy for you, a mis-
sionary's son, to become a Christian ? "

" I wouldn't say it was *easy* ; in fact, I don't
think anyone who has ever really followed the
call of the Master has found it easy.   ' Let him
deny himself, take up his cross, and follow
Me . . . ' was what Christ said, you know."

" Yes, I understand that ; but it must have
been different for a fellow like you from what it
would be for someone like myself ; my people
just don't bother their heads about God. They've
never given me any sort of lead—except in the
art of looking after my own interests."

" Well, it was like this.  I was home in
England during the war.  Chris was at the
school for missionaries' children in that part of
China which the Japanese overran.   That's her
little ' swank ', you may remember."

John nodded.

" I knew all about the way by which one becomes a Christian. We had been brought up on the Bible, as small children. But things were not easy at school, and when I received news of Mother's death I grew bitter and resentful. I hadn't seen her for years ; I wanted to see her again, and I didn't see why she should be taken like that. Then, one day, I happened to be glancing through my Bible, and I read the story of Christ washing the disciples' feet. You may remember that Peter protested and didn't want the Lord to wash his feet. Christ said something like this : ' You don't understand now ; but you will do, later.' I suddenly realized what I was doing. I was putting my wisdom above His. I remembered how He died on the Cross—a seeming failure—and how He rose from the dead, as He had promised. He made all the wise men of His day look foolish ; and I was doing the same as they ! Their trusting in their own wisdom led them so far astray that they crucified Him !

" I fell down on my knees by the side of my bed, thanked Him for showing me my mistake, and yielded to Him my life and my will. Since then I have been learning daily the secret of relying more and more on Him, and not on myself. It is not just a matter of believing the right things about God ; it is taking the right attitude towards Him. The only attitude a

sinful man can take is to own up that he has
failed, and then ask for forgiveness, and a
new start."

John still seemed puzzled. "But don't you
have to *do* something ?   Don't you have to keep
certain rules, go to Church regularly, and all
that ? "

"You don't have to *do* anything ; but if you
really love the Lord Jesus Christ, then you will
*want* to do a number of things—more and more
as time goes by—for the sake of pleasing Him.
That means a great deal more than just going
through a number of routine religious per-
formances."

They were interrupted by the reappearance
of Captain Craven.

"Absolute silence for a quarter of an hour," he
said.   "We're going through Potter Heigham."

Vallin gripped his revolver even more grimly.

Dick and John sat mutely, both of them
wondering whether Hugh would be on the alert,
and would see them pass.

The *Windward* was still moving, though more
slowly, when they heard the sound of sails being
lowered.   Then there was a further noise, which
John guessed was made by the lowering of the
mast.   They looked at each other.   Captain
Craven was not going to stop for anything now.
With the engine throttled back, there was
absolutely no noise, and only very slight vibration
as she slid through the darkness.

" Hope the skipper can see the arch of the road-bridge clearly," thought Dick. " Don't want to pile up against that, whilst we're tied up like registered parcels." The tide was carrying *Windward* steadily along.

There was a moment's bustle and whispering in the well, a slight grating noise, and then quiet again. John and Dick exchanged meaningful looks. Then the vibration began to increase ; they were running out of the ' built-up ' area of riverside bungalows. It was not long before they felt once again the thrust and vibration of the compact but powerful motor. At this rate they would be through Yarmouth well before dawn ; once out in the North Sea, and *Windward* might easily avoid capture. The future looked grim.

## Chapter 15

### HUGH MAKES A TIMELY ARRIVAL

ON board *Sabrina*, a very sleepy-eyed Chris awoke with a strangely guilty feeling. For a few moments she tried in vain to collect her thoughts ; then, suddenly, she realized where she was. Hastily she looked at her watch. It showed the time to be five minutes to six ! She should have radioed Hugh at four o'clock ! But perhaps John and Dick had returned. She took a quick look into the cabin. Her father slept steadily ; the other bunk was empty. She crashed her way into the well, and out through the awning. The dinghy was not there.

Chris hurried back to the cabin, woke her father, and switched on the radio. Hugh would be listening at six o'clock again. There was no point in further secrecy, so she picked up the microphone ; as the hands of her watch moved round to six, she began to speak.

" Hullo, Hugh ! Hullo, Hugh ! Chris calling ; Chris calling. Dick and John not back yet. Dinghy has disappeared. Inform the police. *Windward* may be escaping. Over to you. Please acknowledge."

She switched over to ' Receiving ', but there was no sign of a response. Again she tried ; the air seemed empty.

For a moment she felt lost. What could have happened to Hugh ? If she had not overslept, things might have been very different. But now Dick and John had disappeared and even Hugh had failed.

Mr. Vincent was by now thoroughly awake. Hurriedly she told him the latest news. He looked serious for a moment, and then replied, quietly : " Let's pray about it all."

They both knelt beside the bunk, and there and then committed the whole problem to the Lord Who was so real to them. Chris felt much easier in mind as she got up. She could see no way out of the difficulty, but it was not the first time that, even in her short experience, she had faced what seemed to be a fast-closed door, and had seen it open to the gentle yet mighty push of prayer.

" We must raise the alarm, and then go upstream to see if we can find the dinghy," said Mr. Vincent. " I should think that if we sail a little way upstream, we shall find a footpath which leads to Horsey village. This will save us going back across the Mere. One of us can go in and telephone the police, while the other continues exploring upstream. If you trot into the village, you should have the police on the watch at Yarmouth by six-thirty. That should be time enough ; the wind is not so very strong, and I don't see how they can get through before then."

Without further delay, they hoisted sail and began to edge their way slowly up the New Cut. A clump of bushes made progress slow at first ; the darkness, lightened by the first streaks of dawn, complicated matters.    Suddenly they heard the purr of a motor-boat, which seemed to be coming across Horsey Mere towards them.

" What's this ? " asked Chris.    " More of the *Windward's* gang ? "

" I shouldn't think so ; if they've come across Dick and John, they won't hang about anywhere in these parts."

The motor-launch came steadily nearer ; it was apparently bound for the New Cut, and soon they could see its navigation light coming up astern.    Then it slowed down as its steersman spotted *Sabrina*.    To their surprise they were hailed in a familiar voice :

" *Sabrina* ahoy !    I'm going alongside.    Hold on ! "

" It's Hugh !    Where did he get a motor-boat from ? "

" Hullo there !    Hugh calling ; moor up again, will you ? "

" Right !    We'll tie up by that bush."

*Sabrina's* sails swung loose ; she lost way and turned across stream.    Chris ran forward and tied her up to the stout branch of an overhanging tree.

The motor-boat sputtered alongside ; Chris reached out and grabbed her painter.    Then her engine stopped, and Hugh jumped aboard *Sabrina*.

" My ! I'm glad to see you ! Where are Dick and John ? "

" We don't know ; we're just going to warn the police, and then search up here. They followed the *Windward* along here in the dinghy last night, and we've heard no more. How did you manage to get that motor-boat ? "

" No time for explanations now. Since I did not hear from you at four o'clock as arranged, I thought I'd better come and see for myself. But the first thing is to get the police on the trail. I'll go back across Horsey, and ring them ; you can carry on up the Cut to see what you can find."

" All right ; we'll expect you later. Cheerio for now ! "

" Good-bye ; I shan't be long."

Chris bent down to free the painter as Hugh leaped aboard his new craft. The motor burst into life, noisy against the hush of dawn, and the muddy water was churned up afresh as the launch made off towards Horsey staithe.

## Chapter 16

### THE CHASE BEGINS IN EARNEST

"HULLO, Hullo! Give me the police, please!"

The operator replied in a drowsy voice:

"You want the village policeman, or Yarmouth Headquarters?"

"Yarmouth, please. Hurry, it's urgent!"

"We'll put you through."

Hugh waited impatiently for a few moments.

"Yarmouth police here."

"Officer, I'm ringing from the call-box at Horsey; I can't go into details now. I'm on holiday on the Broads. Two of my friends have disappeared. We had reason to suspect that a yacht which we had met, called the *Windward*, was trying to smuggle out of the country those wanted sabotage experts from Diamatia. My friends followed them up the New Cut last night, and have now disappeared. The yacht has gone also; she may be trying to get out to sea through Yarmouth. Can you stop them? The name of the yacht is *Windward*. It is a single-masted, Bermuda-rigged craft, low built. Her captain is a man named Craven, from Horning. We had some suspicions aroused on Sunday, and even more yesterday."

" It's a pity you didn't tell us before.    How are we to know this isn't a hoax ? "

" I'm afraid you can't tell, at present ; but you can soon check.   I'm sailing on *Viking*, with one of the chaps who has disappeared.   I've left it at Potter Heigham, and come up here in a borrowed motor-launch.   I'm going back now to help my friends who are looking for the missing fellows up the New Cut.   That's where the *Windward* was last seen, about midnight last night."

Hugh added some further details of his position and his plans.   The police officer seemed convinced.

" Very good ; we'll put a watch on the harbour exit at Yarmouth right away.   As a matter of fact we've had some suspicions of that Captain Craven for some time.   For that reason I'm inclined to believe your story.   Will you get in touch with us again as soon as you can ? "

" Right you are ; thanks very much !   I'll ring you again.   If you have a launch which you can send up the New Cut, it would help a lot."

" We may be able to do something ; we'll do what we can."

" Thanks very much ; good-bye for now."

Hugh rang off, and ran back to the staithe where his own launch was moored.   He drove her flat out, harder than she had been driven for many a long day, as he hurried back across the Mere.   The somewhat decrepit engine vibrated and shuddered at the unaccustomed strain, but it kept going, and that was all that Hugh troubled about. The wild beauty of the sunrise might just as well not have been there for all the attention he gave to it. Only one thing possessed his mind ; what would the news be when he met his friends again ? Should he get into touch with John's parents ? What was the best plan of action from now on ? These and similar questions thronged his brain.

He caught up with *Sabrina* just as Mr. Vincent and Chris were tying up by the old mill.

" Any sign of the dinghy ? " he asked.

" Yes ; it's among the reeds, about 200 yards back."

Chris pointed in the direction, and continued : " We didn't stop to get it. We had a good look round, but saw no sign of anyone near it. We did, however, see the marks of fresh foot-prints in the mud along the side of the river bank ; they were facing in this direction. We're just going to explore this mill ; it looks a likely spot for a hide-out. Did you get the police ? "

" Yes ; they're putting a watch on at Yar-mouth. They may also send a launch up here."

" Good ; I don't see how *Windward* could have gone through Yarmouth before dawn ; the wind isn't all that strong, and there are three sets of bridges to pass under."

Hugh thought for a moment, looking reflec-

tively in the direction of his launch.    Suddenly
he broke out :

" But supposing *Windward* should have an
auxiliary motor ? "    The thought had been
suggested by the sight of his own craft.

Chris stopped absolutely still, and then turned
a shade paler.

" We hadn't thought of that !   Oh ! Dad,
perhaps they've got away, with Dick and John
on board ! "

Mr. Vincent's voice remained steady.

" Perhaps they have.   But we mustn't forget
that there is One Who thinks of everything ;
don't leave Him out of the reckoning, Chris."

" Sorry, Dad ; I nearly panicked."

" I'm not surprised ; come and help me look
around here."

The three began their search, their spirits
subdued.

" Looks as if there's been a scrap here," shouted
Hugh, standing by the fence.

The others ran across to him, and saw for
themselves the trampled grass and reeds.

" What's this ?   John's fountain pen ! " Hugh
picked up the easily-identified green pen with
which John had written his letters earlier in their
cruise.

" So they *have* been here.   What's inside the
mill ?   We had better go carefully ! "

They quickly spotted the fresh footmarks in
the muddy doorway ; inside the mill they saw

little sign of human habitation.   Mr. Vincent
noticed that the upper floor was in a quite good
condition, and would have made a splendid
hiding-place for wanted men.

Hugh clambered up by the half-rotten steps.

" Someone's been here all right ! " he shouted
down through the opening in the floor.   " There
are cigarette-ends about ; it looks as if they slept
on a pile of straw in the corner.   I'm coming
down again.   The police or someone can give
this a thorough examination later.   There's
nothing else for me to see."

" Well," said Mr. Vincent, summing up their
discoveries so far, " it looks as if the *Windward*
may have picked up her passengers here.   Then
Dick and John were spotted, and they've been
taken along also.   We can only hope and pray
that they will be stopped at Yarmouth.   Once
they get out to sea, there's no knowing what
these men will do.   If they really are the types
we suspect, they'll have no scruples.   I think
we'd best get back, and try to recover the dinghy."

After a final look round, they made their way
back to where they had spotted the dinghy.
Hugh towed *Sabrina*, to save time, and it was
not long before they were scrambling on the bank,
preparing to rescue the wayward dinghy.   Hugh
and Mr. Vincent soon decided that it would be
necessary for them to wade in mud and water,
so Hugh rolled up his trousers, whilst the others
prepared to help him with a strong pull.   Dick

and John had pushed it well into the reeds when they had abandoned it.

Eventually, Hugh took a length of rope, hitched it on to the stern of the dinghy, and then joined Chris and Mr. Vincent in heaving with all their might and main. The dinghy slid slowly from its muddy bed, and was soon out in clear water again. Hurriedly they searched it, but found no further clues or traces of its former occupants. They were just tying it up to *Sabrina* when they heard the sound of a powerful motor-launch, approaching from the direction of Horsey Mere.

They looked up enquiringly. Was this some ally of the *Windward* ? It was obviously a fast and powerful craft. It was only a very few moments before the stranger came into sight. It was a very smartly-turned-out speedboat, similar in shape and design to those employed by the Royal Air Force during the war. It was dark blue in colour, and had an elaborate wireless aerial system rigged on its short mast.

It drew up smartly alongside *Sabrina*. A police sergeant, who was standing by the controls, called across to Mr. Vincent :

" You're connected with this *Windward* case ? "

" That's right ; Vincent's my name. One of the two missing lads is my son. We've just found their dinghy, and some traces of their presence here and at the old mill yonder."

Mr. Vincent recounted their story, the police

officer listening carefully as they did so.    When he had finished, the sergeant spoke :

"It so happens that we are at Potter Heigham, engaged in testing this new patrol-boat before she is taken over by the Force.    This is a new development, needed because of the heavy holiday traffic on the Broads.    You are providing us with an unexpected trial.    I can't say I like the sound of your story, however.    I'll radio through to find out how things stand now. Stephens ! "

"Yes, Sergeant ? " the radio operator answered from the cabin.

"Contact H.Q., tell them we have met Mr. Vincent, and ask them if there is any further news from Yarmouth of the *Windward*."

"Very good, Sergeant."

"You know," went on the sergeant, "it looks as if you've stumbled on something pretty important.    That man Craven disappeared during the war ; he was suspected of subversive activities.    We've had half an eye on him since his return home, but we've never had anything definite to pin on to him.    That boat of his is a very smart craft.    We rather think that she has an auxiliary motor.    Just before war broke out, in 1939, there was one incident which aroused a lot of suspicion.    A powerful wireless transmitter was used occasionally by someone in this area, transmitting code messages which no-one could decipher.    It was always done during

THE CHASE BEGINS IN EARNEST

the holiday rush-period, however, when there were so many yachts about that we just could not get a definite line on it. Once or twice *Windward* went on long trips in the North Sea ; looking back, it's easy to see that he may well have been smuggling agents into and out of the country. And from what you say, he is the chap with the radio. Well, Stephens ? "

" H.Q. says that nothing has been seen at Yarmouth. An officer has also been posted at Acle Bridge to make doubly certain. A fisherman at Yarmouth says he thought he heard the sound of a muffled exhaust at about five o'clock. The guard at Customs control point say that they are quite certain nothing has got past them."

" Thank you, constable. Keep constant radio watch. You might also keep one ear on the waveband used by the *Windward* ; I expect this gentleman can supply you with that ? "

Hugh gave the required figure right away, and the constable disappeared again into his cabin.

Sergeant McIver turned to Mr. Vincent.

" Well, sir, we'll come back and have a look at the mill, if you don't mind. Then I think the best plan will be for you to make your way back to Potter Heigham, and stay on your boat there until we get further news. We shall know where to find you if you do that."

" Yes, Sergeant ; I think you're right. Shall we walk along the bank ? It seems to have been the way the boys went ; we may find some more evidence there."

" Good idea ; I don't want to take our launch any farther along here ; this channel is none too deep. It is actually a disused canal, and a little farther on it is completely overgrown."

Sergeant McIver and Mr. Vincent moved off along the bank ; Hugh offered to stay with Chris, who, partly as a result of the strain, and partly because of fatigue, said she would prefer to rest for a while in the cabin.   She would then make a start with preparing the breakfast.

Hugh adopted as sympathetic an attitude as possible, sitting on the bunk on the starboard side of the cabin, while Chris lay resting on the other bunk.   For a few moments there was silence ; then Chris reached along the shelf which ran beside the bunk, and fetched out a small leather-bound book.  She found her place, looked at it for a few moments, and then said :

" Would you join me in a word of prayer, Hugh ?   I do feel that this is the sort of difficulty which is best faced with God's help, don't you ? "

Hugh hesitated ; he had to give an honest answer, and did not find that an easy thing to do.

" To be quite frank, Chris, I'm afraid I don't know much about it ; not from experience, that is.   I must say I'm pretty worried ; I don't look forward to explaining things to John's people, I know that ; even if he *was* technically the senior of the two of us. I'm certainly willing to try praying, if you will lead. It's not quite in my line . . . yet."

Even as he spoke, he became aware that his speech was a somewhat lame affair ; the attitude to God which he had previously adopted, and which had always seemed so smart and up to date when he shared it with his like-minded friends, now seemed a poor and almost pitiable thing. He realized that he was confessing that there had been a big gap in his life ; he had been missing something very important—perhaps more important than anything else in the world.

Chris began to pray. Simply, quietly, and with an air of complete confidence, she named her need before God ; not in vague, general terms, but with precise detail. Hugh also noticed that she did not begin by straightway mentioning the things she wanted : she began with words of thankfulness for things which had happened favourably ; for the timely arrival of Hugh and of the police ; and also for the promises of God's Word, in which she seemed to find cause for complete confidence in God's willingness to hear and to help.

Hugh listened thoughtfully ; he was deeply impressed. He had read a few religious books, and had heard a limited selection of sermons, mostly on school Founder's Days and similar formal occasions. He was familiar with the stock arguments with which he and his friends put off

11

the whole idea of facing the challenge of Christ personally. But here, in this movingly simple prayer, and in the whole atmosphere of the Vincents' lives, was something which made his clever arguments look cheap and nasty ; mere tinsel, shown up for what it was when true gold was set alongside of it. Whatever else could be done, this sort of Christianity could not be sneered away or laughed off.

Chris finished her prayer ; Hugh muttered an echoing " Amen." Then she turned, looked him straight in the face, and asked him a disarmingly simple question.

" Why isn't prayer in your line, Hugh ? It's like a good many things in life—you shouldn't condemn them until you know something about them, trying them for yourself if necessary. But there's this difference ; once you have really learned the way of prayer for yourself, you never want to do without it again."

" Oh, well ; I suppose it's because I've just taken other people's opinions for granted. I must say that I feel a good deal calmer and easier in mind as a result of that prayer. But I feel rather guilty of cashing in on something which I don't really deserve. I can't expect God to start organizing aid for me when I've left Him out of the reckoning for so long."

" It's surprising how mercifully He deals with us, Hugh. But perhaps we can talk about that later. It's time to get the breakfast going. We

mustn't make prayer an excuse for dodging the
' daily round '."

Hugh, Chris and Mr. Vincent joined together
in a somewhat cheerless breakfast. Though there
was no outward sign of despair or even gloom,
they were all feeling the burden of concern, and
did not attempt to hide those feelings beneath a
thin pretence of joking. Mr. Vincent could not
help chiding himself for not calling the police in
sooner. But, as the sergeant had pointed out,
things had happened so quickly that they had
had little time in which to make up their minds
without any trace of doubt.

" By the way, Hugh," said Chris, " you have
not told us how you got hold of that motor-
launch."

" That's soon explained. I saw the owner of
the boatyard when I arrived last evening. I
thought that perhaps I might want to get up
here in a hurry, so I had a word with him about
hiring the launch, which was moored up near
*Viking*. He said that I could have it at any time ;
apparently it is seldom wanted at this time of the
year, but he keeps it in going order for the benefit
of occasional fishing-parties which come out here
for the day. I shall have to settle up with him
when we get back."

" It has certainly proved very useful," said
Mr. Vincent. " You will also be able to tow us
down Meadow Dyke. The wind seems to have

shifted somewhat, and we should have a hard job without such help."

" I'll be glad to do it. But the police-launch would be faster. She is a beauty ! "

" Yes ; I wonder if there is any more news ? "

" I'll slip across and see about it while you're clearing away."

## Chapter 17

### JOHN GETS A SEVERE SHOCK

AFTER they passed through Potter Heigham, Dick and John were allowed to talk again, though only in whispers ; Vallin seemed sullenly resentful of their having even this privilege.

Their prospects certainly seemed dim. They kept off any discussion of their own plight, knowing that Vallin was listening, and would pick up any clue they might chance to give in the course of conversation.

After giving them this permission to talk, Captain Craven had returned to the well ; but he did not stay there long, for it was now plain sailing until they reached the strongly tidal stretch of river below Acle Bridge. He therefore returned to the cabin, and seemed to be in a better frame of mind.

" You may as well know the programme," he said. " You can't do anything about it, whatever happens. We should pass Acle Bridge at 4.30, and then we shall get through Yarmouth well before six. I am not quite sure how I shall deal with you after that. I think the best thing would be for you to be set adrift in the dinghy when we are well out into the North Sea. We'll send a radio message to let your friends know what has happened to you ; we don't want to pile up unnecessary charges.   We may, of course, be forced to take you farther—that will make things more difficult ; we shall have to wait and see."

"I suppose we should be grateful for small mercies," replied John, quietly.

"You should indeed ; if these passengers of mine had their way, your corpses would have been settling down in the mud of Horsey Mere by now.   Of course, they are not likely to mutiny, since they depend so much on me for navigation ; but I can't make any promises ! "

"But you hav'n't a chance of getting across the North Sea," suggested John, hopefully.

"We have thought of all that, surprisingly enough," was the reply.   "This boat was never intended to carry us very far ; if you had not interfered, the other passengers would have been transferred to another craft, and we should have returned to Yarmouth the same day, having enjoyed a short pleasure cruise in the North Sea.   I do not propose to tell you what sort of craft would have picked them up ; you must guess that."

"There's plenty of Diamatian merchant ship-ping about," suggested John.

"Possibly," said Captain Craven, with a faint smile.   "Anyhow, it looks as if we shall find out before very long.   By the way, I said I would be kind enough to radio a message to your friends if I have to set you adrift ; is there any special time at which they would be more likely to hear me ? "

John thought for a moment. There would be no harm in telling him at this stage in the adventure. Then he spoke up: "Well, they may not bother to listen, now that we have gone ; but if they do, six, eight, and ten o'clock this morning would be the best times."

There followed some minutes of silence. Captain Craven had lit a cigarette, and was taking his ease on one of the bunks.

Suddenly Dick broke the silence.

" There's one thing you have not allowed for."

" What do you mean ? " asked Captain Craven.

" The possibility of our having arranged for a warning to be given early if we failed to return to *Sabrina*."

John looked at Dick in amazement, which rapidly turned to anger. This was giving the whole game away ! What could Dick be thinking of ? He frowned as heavily as he could, but Dick continued, apparently heedless of his companion's grimaces.

" You are not perfect, you know, Captain Craven ; you should credit us with a little more common sense."

" I don't quite understand. I hope you have not been so foolish as to make things more

difficult for us. It will prove a costly business
for you, if you have."

"As a matter of fact," persisted Dick, still
ignoring the fierce frown which now seemed
to have fixed itself upon John's features, " we
have made just such arrangements. You may
possibly get past Acle Bridge, though even that
is doubtful. You will certainly not get past
Yarmouth. We arranged for the alarm to be
raised at 4 a.m. Very soon after that hour
there will be watchers at Acle and at Yarmouth.
You can't possibly get through if someone is
on the look-out ; your only hope is to slip through
in the darkness unnoticed. You might just
as well give in right away ! "

John looked as if he could have torn Dick's
tongue out. He could not restrain himself.
He cried out fiercely :

"You idiot, Dick! Fancy giving the game away
like that ! I really thought you had more sense."

" Sorry, John, old man," came the even-voiced
reply, " I'll explain later. You'll have to take
it on trust for the moment."

John did not look at all satisfied ; he slumped
back, and appeared to have lost interest in the
whole proceedings.

Captain Craven, on the other hand, was
obviously greatly affected by this new information. " How will your friends raise the alarm ? "
he asked abruptly. " Have they got a private
telephone on *Sabrina* ? "

"No, but they've John's radio transmitter; it has been repaired, and it is powerful enough to land you in trouble quite soon now!"

"You mean that you transferred it to *Sabrina*?"

"That's right."

Captain Craven's tone changed from his former easy-going bantering style.

"You young fiends! You're a sight too clever for your ages! I wish I had taken the advice which Vallin here has been so persistently giving me! However, I thank you for the information. I would have you know that you also may not have thought of everything. Beware of gloating too soon, my young friends!"

With that he hurried out into the well, and began a low-toned, almost whispered conversation with the man at the helm. John and Dick tried in vain to hear what was being said.

They had not been forbidden to speak to each other, but the effect of Dick's unexpected interruption had been to make John keep his mouth firmly closed, this being the most forceful way he had of showing his complete disapproval of Dick's action. Dick seemed content to let it be so, and sat quietly back, his eyes closed, almost as if he were asleep.

Captain Craven called out to their watchful guard: "Vallin! Put one of the others in charge of the boys, and come out here, will you?" Vallin made his way outside and joined in the discussion. Dick's information had evidently given the crew of the *Windward* some food for serious thought. The other passengers remained in the cabin, but were saying very little ; when they did speak it was in a foreign language, and so quickly that neither Dick nor John could catch more than an odd word here and there. A dark shadow seemed to brood over the strangely-assorted company ; the atmosphere was tense indeed.

It was not long before Vallin returned to the cabin. Whatever had been the decision reached by the conference in the well, he obviously did not feel too happy about it. He resumed his sullen watch, taking the revolver from his companion again. If anything, he looked even more malevolent than before, as he kept his scowling gaze grimly fixed on his prisoners.

Just after his return, the vibration of the motor increased still further ; it was obvious that the *Windward* was now being driven all out. Captain Craven seemed determined to make a desperate bid for the open waters of the North Sea ; John and Dick exchanged looks. John obviously felt angry at Dick's having told of their arrangements ; Dick remained quiet, without offering any explanation, The fact was that he could not make such an explanation, because it would have meant giving away to the enemy his reasons for so unexpectedly speaking up. The tension in the cabin grew steadily greater.

## Chapter 18

### HUGH RECEIVES A MESSAGE

THE police had no fresh news for the Vincents when Hugh enquired, as he had promised to do. Nothing had been seen, either at Acle or at Yarmouth. It was now daylight, and it looked as if *Windward* had given them all the slip.

The police authorities had made contact with security officials in London, and, as a result, aircraft were preparing to begin a sea search for the missing yacht. Flying conditions were quite good, visibility was fair, so that there was real hope of their being successful.

There was nothing further which the Vincents could do at this stage in the search, and so they cleared up *Sabrina*, and were soon being towed across Horsey Mere towards Potter Heigham. They had arranged with the police that they would stay there, so that immediate contact could be made with them if and when necessary. They could use the phone from one of the boat-yards for that purpose.

Hugh was at the tiller of the motor-launch, keeping a watchful eye on the rather slender rope which was doing duty as a tow-line. They were nearing the narrow entrance to Meadow Dyke when he suddenly turned his head and called back to Chris, who was busy mopping the foredeck of *Sabrina* :

"Hullo there, Chris ! Could you take over here for a few minutes ? I've had a thought ; it might be a good idea to tune in on the *Windward's* wavelength and listen for a while, in case she should be transmitting. The police-launch may be busy on some other message, and we might pick something up which they would miss."

The exchange was soon made. Hugh explained the few simple controls to Chris, and jumped back to *Sabrina*. He dived into the cabin, turned on the radio, and waited quietly. Just before eight o'clock, there was a hum, as of a transmitter warming up. Almost immediately afterwards there was a short series of staccato morse signals. It was a very brief message, and in volume it was considerably softer than the messages which they had previously heard ; this was probably because the transmitter was now much farther away. The message stopped, and the transmitter was immediately switched off. Hugh transcribed it for Mr. Vincent's benefit :

'Boys adrift North Sea. *Windward.*'

Hastily Hugh switched the set over to the 'Transmit' position, and sent a similarly abrupt message :

'Message received. *Sabrina.*' He repeated it in order to make doubly sure, remarking as he did so :

" This is a fairly weak transmitting outfit, so that they may not get the reply. But it was worth trying. I assume that they sent only a short message because they were afraid that we might fix their position with a directional aerial. It doesn't sound too good."

" No ! It's a good thing that that police-launch is following us ; we can pass the news on to them at once."

This was soon done, for the launch was coming up behind them as they were receiving the message ; the police, in their turn, forwarded the message direct to their H.Q. The search planes could now be given a more definite briefing.

Once again the Vincents settled down to patient waiting. They reached Potter Heigham at a quarter past nine, and Hugh hastened to return the motor-boat to the owner, and settle the account for its hire. When he explained a little of what had been happening, the owner was sympathetically interested. He said that he hoped to have *Viking* patched up by that same evening.

*Sabrina* was moored up securely next to the *Viking*, on which the carpenters were already busy. Mr. Vincent suggested that Hugh should transfer his gear from *Viking*, as there was a vacant bunk on *Sabrina*, and they did not want to have to run backwards and forwards. Besides, the radio was best kept on *Sabrina* until *Viking* was in commission again, and Hugh would be needed if it became necessary to use it again. While this transfer was being made, Chris went to the stores, close by the bridge, in order to replenish food-supplies. Mr. Vincent and Hugh followed her, having decided that it was time to inform John's parents of what had happened. They rang the police H.Q. at Yarmouth, and arranged for a message to be sent to that effect.

When these arrangements had been satisfactorily made, water-tanks had been refilled, and all needful jobs completed, they gathered in *Sabrina's* cabin, and reviewed the whole exciting story of the preceding twenty-four hours.

There seemed little doubt that *Windward* had escaped, and that their friends were in serious danger ; there was plainly nothing further that they could do ; theirs was the harder part— waiting for news which might not come, and which they could do nothing to improve or hasten. Nor were they looking forward to meeting John's parents, who would probably be arriving some time that afternoon.

" We have made it a matter of prayer," said Mr. Vincent. " There's nothing more we can do ; we must not worry now. If we believe anything at all, we believe that we have done the most important thing of all, and that the matter is now in the hands of Him Who is all-wise and all-powerful. Let us rest in that fact.

I am going to catch up with some of my arrears of correspondence."

Chris went into her forward cabin to clean up ; Hugh went ashore to watch the carpenters at work on *Viking*. He got into conversation with the old craftsman who was in charge, picked up some incidental but useful information about ships and their construction, learned a little about the history of the *Viking*, and also that the job would definitely be finished that evening.

He was still keeping up this conversation when a powerful car pulled up in the yard outside the owner's office. Out of it stepped a high-ranking police officer ("A Superintendent, at least," thought Hugh), together with two other men, in civilian dress, but with a plainly military bearing.

" Is Mr. Vincent about, please ? "

" Yes," replied Hugh, " I'll take you to him ; he's on board *Sabrina* here."

The group of men moved towards *Sabrina*, but Mr. Vincent heard their voices as they approached, and put his head enquiringly outside the cabin doors.

" Good afternoon, gentlemen ; please come on board," he said, seeing who they were.

When they had seated themselves along one side of the cabin, causing the yacht to take a noticeable list, for they were powerfully-built men, they introduced themselves.

The police officer spoke first : " I'm Superintendent Parker, of the Norfolk Constabulary. These are two officers of the Security Service ; they have flown up from London, and are anxious to learn all they can about this mysterious yacht with which you seem to have become rather dramatically involved."

They began straight away, firing a string of questions at Mr. Vincent, who, prompted by Chris and Hugh, was able to give them a clear picture of what had happened. The officers allowed no detail to slip their notice, and they took nothing for granted. Once or twice, when some point was mentioned, they looked knowingly at one another, as if it was something which they had half expected to hear. When the story had been completely told, they both looked very serious. One of them spoke :

" It certainly seems that they've got away, Mr. Vincent. There is some very nasty trouble brewing, and these are the last men whom we would have desired to escape. However, I must say that John and Hugh here have shown remarkable keenness in getting on to their trail. It may yet be that the interference caused by the lads will prove to be the one bit of sand which will wreck the smoothly-oiled wheels of their organization. They have plenty of money and other facilities ; there is even some suggestion of a submarine operating as part of the organiza- tion. If there is any truth in that, we may yet see your boy turning up with his friend on the

Continent somewhere, though I rather doubt if they would like him to learn so much about their set-up. However, we may yet hope for better news. We'll keep in close touch with you. I think we'll go and explore that windmill."

" Very good. We'll be here if we're wanted. You can't miss the mill ; it is the first one you come to, sailing up the New Cut from Horsey Mere."

## Chapter 19

### THINGS LOOK VERY SERIOUS

JOHN'S parents arrived at Potter Heigham at teatime. They were very agitated, and insisted on hearing the story several times over, hoping to gain some crumb of comfort out of this repetition. They were rather inclined to blame Mr. Vincent, though they could see his point of view.

When the police officers called in again, Mr. and Mrs. Wilson badgered them for full details of any theories which they might have, what they were doing by way of a search, and what they thought of future possibilities. The police did their best to reassure them, but they were in no mood to take the word of another ; they appeared to want to check everything for themselves, and it was a very harried police officer who later made his escape from their cross-questioning.

While all this was going on, Hugh sat quietly back, comparing the very different attitudes adopted by the Vincents and the Wilsons. Both families were facing similar tragic possibilities. A stranger coming into the cabin, without knowing the full story, would never have guessed as much, however ; the Wilsons were restless, fretful and fussy ; they talked almost continually, though by now their conversation was mere repetition, going round in familiar and gloomy circles. The Vincents were calm and quiet ; they seemed to be inwardly at ease, in spite of the strain. They were willing to take the police officer's word that everything possible was being done ; their bearing was that of people with a secret cause for confidence ; they faced the possible disaster as those who had already overcome its sting.

" I don't know what I shall do if anything happens to John," said Mrs. Wilson, at the end of one of her long, rambling, and quite aimless reviews of events. " I feel quite desperate ; it is the uncertainty that is so frightful ; we may never know what has happened ; that would be too terrible for words ! Don't you agree, Mr. Vincent ? "

Mr. Vincent replied in his usual quiet tones.

" Quite frankly, no, Mrs. Wilson, I can't say that I do. Chris and I cannot feel like that about Dick. We are united in bonds which no power on earth can break ; not even death can really divide us. Chris and Dick and their mother and I are united in the love of Christ ; nothing can separate us from Him, and nothing can bring that love to an end. Whatever happens to Dick, we know that the Saviour Whom we have learned to trust without question is with Him ; and whether in life or death, Dick is with his Master. We couldn't wish for more than that ! "

The Wilsons looked somewhat uncomfortable ; this was a new language to them ; they were out of their depth.

" Er . . . Oh, yes, I see . . . I didn't exactly mean it in that way . . ." began Mrs. Wilson, hesitantly.

" I know you didn't ; but I answered like that, because to me the most important truth of all is the one I have tried to explain.  I know you won't mind my speaking frankly, but I do feel that it is a great pity that so many people, parents and children, drift along through life without giving these things so much as a thought. This world is full of uncertainties, and there is little enough in this life on which you can find a solid foothold ; it's all right when things are going smoothly and well ; but a great liner needs lifeboats as well as a swimming pool ; and a man needs something which will carry him through the dark valleys ; it's easy enough on the sunlit uplands.   We have found that something in the everlasting love of God, made real to us through Jesus Christ."

For a moment there was no answer.   Then, just as Mr. Wilson was about to make some reply, Chris, who had been outside in the boatyard, came in with a message.

" The police have just phoned through to say that the latest sea searches have been without result.   They'll soon have to call them off for today.   The  authorities are very puzzled about it all, as they have had an extra large force at work.  It begins to look as if the submarine has been in use, and the *Windward* has possibly been scuttled."

Faces already long fell even further at this news.  A fresh flow of futile comment was about to break out from Mrs. Wilson when they were interrupted by the sound of the approach of the police-launch, which was returning from the New Cut, carrying the Police Superintendent, together with the two Security officials.

The Superintendent came on board *Sabrina* to give them the latest news :

" We've just heard from H.Q. that they have drawn a blank today ; I gather that you have also heard the news.  I think I can tell you a little more about the whole scheme, though much of what I say is strictly confidential, you under-stand."  The others nodded.  He continued, " We have reason to believe that the *Windward* has already made one, if not two, successful trips this season.  A man who was a notorious agent, and who had been deported from this country, suddenly turned up in the Durham coalfield a month or so ago.  He is so well known that it seems impossible that he should have come in through any ordinary channel, even disguised."

" What beats me," said Mr. Wilson, thought-fully, " is how an Englishman like Craven can get mixed up with a crowd like that.  It can hardly be money he's after."

" It doesn't need to be," observed Mr. Vincent. " The trouble with Diamatia is that she has lost her soul ; she has gone after false gods. That disease is catching, and can infect an Englishman as easily as it can any other nationality. England, in fact, is showing many symptoms of the same disease today."

Mr. Wilson looked shocked. " What do you mean by that ? " he demanded, rather curtly.

" Only that when the Bible is neglected in the homes and hearts of a nation, that nation will sooner or later fall under the influence of evil spiritual forces—as Germany did, and as Diamatia is doing."

Further discussion was cut short by the departure of the Superintendent. The Wilsons followed soon after, having arranged to stay at a hotel in Yarmouth where they could keep in the closest possible touch with the authorities.

Darkness began to close in ; the river flowed coldly and sluggishly past, grey-brown in colour under the cloudy sky. Several times they heard an aircraft droning overhead (" Possibly been looking for Dick and John," observed Christine. " They ought to find some trace of them—unless the message was a fake, to draw off attention while they made good their escape to Diamatia.")

Mr. Vincent sat writing by the light of the small electric light with which *Sabrina's* cabin was equipped. Hugh was reading—an absorbingly interesting book which the Vincents had lent

him, and which gave him a series of shocks.
It made it clear that the scientists who attacked
Christianity so loudly were themselves bigoted
and prejudiced men, as blind as anyone else to
those truths which did not fit into their scheme of
things. Hugh had always looked up to them as
men of careful thought and balanced judgment ;
he now saw that some of his ' idols ' were themselves guilty of serious errors and shallow, biassed
thinking. The book made out a strong case
for Christianity, facing the difficulties fairly
and squarely, and Hugh slowly came to see that
he had never given the subject proper thought.
He began to suspect that one reason for this was
the fact that it made him feel rather uncomfortable ; he was not, after all, the fine type that he
had imagined himself to be. Perhaps that was
why some of the enemies of Christianity had
turned against it so bitterly. They didn't like
it because it hurt their pride.

Whilst his thoughts were following this line,
Chris, who had been busy in the well, preparing
a bumper supper, began to sing softly. Hugh
caught occasional snatches of the words of the
chorus she was singing :

> *Only to be what He wants me to be*
> *Every moment of every day ;*
> *Yielded completely to Jesus alone*
> *Every step of this pilgrim way . . .*

' This pilgrim way ' . . . the word ' pilgrim '
flooded his mind with associations, for he had

spent a holiday hiking along the track of the
mediæval pilgrims as it followed the North
Downs.   He remembered how there had always
been in their minds as they made the journey the
thought that they were aiming at a goal—the
ancient shrine of Canterbury.   Each night they
lodged for a few hours in a hostel, but nowhere
did they stay for longer than a night.   They were
passing on, moving through the towns and
villages, looking for a famous city.   But the true
meaning of it had escaped him at the time.
Now, recalling Mr. Vincent's recent words to
the Wilsons, it became clearer.   Nothing fixed
in this life. . . . Living like pilgrims, aiming at
something greater, something beyond, something
enduring, clean and pure.   This made sense ;
Hugh found it attractive.   He began to long
that he, too, might share the Vincents' secret.
He would ask them some more about it when the
opportunity came.

The evening meal, set out neatly in the cosiness
of the dark-timbered cabin, was not in any way
a hilarious affair ; a subdued note ran through
all their conversation.   Yet there was again that
marked absence of fretfulness or strain ; once
more Hugh found himself admiring and envying
their poise and calm.   In the back of his mind
there lingered the picture of the Wilsons, noisily
fussing, obviously worried, trying to drown their
distress beneath a flood of futile words.   He
much preferred his present companions.

After supper, Hugh and Chris washed up, and then went to the boatyard to make a final call to police H.Q. Nothing more had been seen or heard ; a complete blank had been drawn. There was nothing they could do.

They had decided on going to bed early, and Chris quickly disappeared into her cabin, after they had joined together in a time of prayer, and Mr. Vincent had read some words of encouragement and hope from the Epistle to the Romans.

Hugh was ready for sleep. No sooner had he laid himself down on the well-sprung bunk than he was in a deep sleep. Apart from a tantalizing dream, in which he had arranged to pilot an aircraft in a search for some lost seaman, but for one trivial reason after another was prevented from taking off, he enjoyed a night of untroubled rest.

## Chapter 20

### HUGH HAS AN INSPIRATION

IT was during prayers, after breakfast the
following morning, that Hugh had his in-
spiration. The thought had actually come to
him while Mr. Vincent was praying—but he had
not interrupted until they had finished, and were
preparing to clear away. In fact, he was tempted
at first to dismiss the thought altogether, as being
too absurd to mention. But it had persisted
and grown in force of conviction, so that he did
not hesitate to share it.

" Mr. Vincent ! I've had an idea ! It sounds
unlikely, but it is just possible ; and if there is
anything in it, it gives us fresh hope. It came to
me whilst you were praying just now."

Mr. Vincent looked interested. " What's the
brain wave, Hugh ? "

" Yes, come on, share the good news," asked
Chris, eagerly.

" Supposing *Windward* hasn't gone out to sea
at all ! "

" What do you mean ? "

" Well, it's very strange that no trace of her or
the dinghy has been seen. It appears that
several squadrons of R.A.F. planes have been
on the look-out, besides fishing craft and other
vessels."

" Yes, but she's only a boat."

" I know ; but she couldn't have gone very far
—that restricts the area to be searched. And I've
just remembered something that may explain
her disappearance. This is not the first time that
she has disappeared. You remember I told
you that one of the first things which drew our
attention to her was that she passed us on Saturday evening, this side of Horning, travelling
downstream. Then although we had not seen
her in the meantime, she passed us again, still
travelling in the same direction, on the Sunday
morning. This meant that either she had turned
round, during the night, and gone upstream,
and then turned again to pass us (which seems
pointless) ; or else she had some sort of hiding-
place along that stretch of river. Then we could
have passed her without noticing her. We went
down into Ranworth Broad and out again, and
that was the only possible ' side-turning ' down
which she could have gone, for she passed us in
that stretch of river between the entrance to
Ranworth and St. Benet's Abbey. There was
no sign of her in Ranworth."

" Quite a speech, Hugh ; but I think I follow."

" Well then ; to come to Monday morning.
Suppose Captain Craven had not been certain of
getting through Yarmouth before the alarm was
raised ; he may have found out that we planned
to raise it at four o'clock. He would realize
that there would be no chance of escaping, once

the authorities were on the watch, since his passengers were so important that a very careful search would be made as soon as the news was known. It's more than a matter of Dick and John, after all. He might then decide not to run the gauntlet at Yarmouth. He could instead make his way upstream, up the Bure, get to his hiding-place before dawn, and then lie low. When the hue and cry had died down, he would have another try at getting out to sea."

" That's quite an idea, Hugh. But what about that radio message which said that the boys were adrift ? "

" I'm coming to that. It's a bit of a difficulty, I know. But there's this possibility. It was a very short message, so that it would have been almost impossible to get a position-fix from it. That may have been to put the sea-searchers off the scent ; or even more important, to keep us from finding out that he was not at sea at all. The signal was softer, I admit ; but that could easily have been done deliberately in order to make the deception more complete. It's the sort of thing that Captain Craven would be very likely to do."

Mr. Vincent nodded thoughtfully. Then, quite quickly, his mind was made up.

" I somehow think you're right," he said. " We must get in touch with the police at once. I think their launch is still moored up nearby.

If not, we shall have to ring them as before. We ourselves will prepare to sail at once in order to join in the search.  We can borrow *Viking's* dinghy ; there's no point in bringing *Viking* herself, is there ? "

" None at all," replied Hugh, his excitement visibly growing.  " I'll go and inform the police —I expect I shall have something of a job to persuade them to consider my suggestion. Their launch is moored up just over the other side of the bridge, if I remember rightly.  I'll get along now.  Be back soon ! "

With that, Hugh ran along the river bank, across the road, and down to the mooring where the police-launch was tied up, bright with new varnish.  The Sergeant listened carefully to his suggestion, and then fetched out the charts so that they could get some idea of possible hide-aways.  It was easy to fix limits, as Hugh had a good idea of where their Saturday-night mooring place had been, and also where the *Windward* had passed them on the Sunday. The police sergeant did not seem too unwilling to believe Hugh's story ; the failure of the search-planes had surprised the authorities ; they were ready to listen to a new and possible suggestion. They were soon in radio contact with H.Q., and there was a promise of several launches and also a land search party.

" You had better not go searching about without any weapons," said Sergeant McIver, on hearing of the Vincents' plans. " Can you handle a revolver ? "

" We had a course of instruction during last term's cadet camp. I should certainly feel happier with one handy," said Hugh.

Sergeant McIver handed him a small but useful weapon, giving him very careful instructions about not making use of it unless absolutely necessary, and then preferably for intimidation purposes only.

When he returned to *Sabrina*, he found that the Vincents had indeed been busy. Breakfast had been cleared away ; the awning which was drawn over the well at night had been folded and stowed in the tabernacle ready for moving off.

There was no sign of a break in the clouds, which were being driven rapidly across the sky by a steady south-west wind. It was cool, but good weather for sailing ; and that was all that mattered just then. With Hugh's help the mast was quickly lowered, they quanted *Sabrina* down-stream, under the railway bridge, and then through the narrow arch of the brick-built road bridge. The passage of the latter was particularly tricky, as the tide was turning, and the wind was strong enough to swing *Sabrina's* hull well off the desired course. Hugh proved himself to be a vigorous wielder of the quant pole however, and they were soon moored up on the other side, where they hoisted sail with all speed.

While Mr. Vincent and Hugh were busy with this latter manœuvre, Chris had gone to the stores to collect provisions. She returned just as they were ready to set sail again. Once they had cast off, they found the wind to be more than sufficient for their needs. (" In fact, if we were not in a hurry, I'd order a reef to be taken in the mainsail," observed Mr. Vincent.) They had to tack downstream for about half a mile, dead into the teeth of the wind. This was an exciting business. As she turned at the end of each cross-river tack, *Sabrina* hesitated, like a bather on the brink of a pool, and then plunged over on to the other tack, heeling sharply and rapidly gaining speed. Loose items of equipment rattled and slid from side to side in the cabin and the lockers. Then, as she started to get into her stride, she had to be swung over to the opposite tack, and began the process over again. The wind was gusty, so that once or twice she was hit by a heavy squall just as she was on the turn. This caused her to heel over alarmingly, dipping her deck beneath the water ; but she quickly recovered, and set off furiously on another sprint for the opposite bank.

Hugh had become sufficiently accustomed to this process to enjoy it thoroughly. Mr. Vincent was very clearly the master of this lively craft, and Chris and Hugh sat in the well, hair blowing wildly in the wind, the excitement of the chase adding to the thrill of fast sailing.

Soon they had rounded the bend, just past the narrow dyke which leads to Womack Water, and they were now able to sail close to the wind on a straight course down the river, without having to tack. They were moving swiftly along, and settled down to a good stretch of plain but exciting sailing. They opened the chart again, went over the ground carefully, and discussed the most likely places for the *Windward's* lair.

Hugh had marked out the possible area with a pencil; it was a useful stretch from Captain Craven's point of view, including as it did the marshy, reed-covered area between the mouth of the River Ant and Horning Ferry.

"There are several side-streams or lagoons marked," said Hugh, "in addition to the dyke which leads down to Ranworth Broad. For about a mile and a half there is continuous marsh, extending up to a mile from the edge of the river. I was reading somewhere that it had been open water at one time, but that the reeds had gradually extended their hold, until now only the river channel remains. There seems to be practically no solid ground in that area."

"No," said Mr. Vincent, "only mud and reeds. In places the mud is several feet deep; elsewhere it is only a few inches below the water surface. It would be an ideal place for a secret mooring if you could work out some way of getting into the reeds without leaving your way of entrance clearly to be seen by other people. It will need all our powers of observation to find the yacht. And there's always the thought that there may be nothing there."

"Yes," observed Chris, "but there's the encouragement which comes from being able to do something ; there's nothing worse than having to wait helplessly while others get on with the search."

"I agree," added Mr. Vincent, "and what's more, I have a feeling that there is a great deal in Hugh's suggestion. I can't help thinking of the moment at which the thought first came to him. I don't think that was an accident. It may be that today will see the end of the search."

"I sincerely hope so," replied Hugh. "Although plain cruising around will seem very tame after this ! "

"Tame, yes ; but none the less pleasant for all that ! "

*Sabrina* was now making very good progress, and soon rounded the big bend in the river by Thurne mouth. The next stretch of river, up the Bure towards St. Benet's Abbey, was made with the wind on the port beam ; *Sabrina* revelled in such conditions, and drove swiftly through the water. Whilst they were on this section, the police launch from Potter Heigham came alongside for a while, so that Mr. Vincent and Sergeant

13

McIver could exchange notes and make plans.

The police had been informed that two light observation aircraft had been detailed to assist in the search, and they would be in radio communication with the police launch. The first thing to be done was to make a quick survey of the whole area as seen from the main waterway ; detailed search could then follow that up if no clues had been found.

" Perhaps your young friend would come aboard and help us with this first look-round," suggested Sergeant McIver. " We will arrange to meet you if we do not see anything, and he can then return to continue the hunt with you. Another pair of sharp eyes will be of great help in our first quick search."

Hugh was in enthusiastic agreement with the suggestion. He leapt on board, and waved a cheery farewell as the powerful motors accelerated and the launch surged smoothly forward, leaving *Sabrina* rocking in her wake. The police launch was a beautiful piece of craftsmanship, with high-powered motors which were capable of lifting her almost clean out of the water as she tore ahead. They hummed steadily now as she drove quickly onwards.

" It was about here that the *Windward* passed us the second time," said Hugh, just after they had passed the mouth of the River Ant. " If there is a hide-out, it is between here and the end of Ward Marsh."

" Right," answered Sergeant McIver. " Keep your eyes skinned ! " He reduced speed as he said this. " The left bank is the more likely one ; most of the marshes are on that side ; we'll concentrate there going upstream, and then we can cover the other side when we return. We'll also explore any side-channels as we go."

The three men gazed steadily at the reed-filled marshes as they passed along ; wild, wind-tossed expanses of reeds, with here and there a clump of bushes and an occasional tree, were all they could see.

" We can't rely on spotting the *Windward's* mast," remarked the sergeant. " They would almost certainly have lowered it. They have probably got plenty of supplies on board, and, by boiling the water, they can be self-sufficient for a good many days. We'll go down here ; this leads to Ranworth Broad. The public part is quite small, but there is quite a large private section. That is barred by a strong boom, however. This is just the sort of section where a quiet hide-away might be situated ; keep an extra sharp look-out."

They cruised slowly down the tree-lined channel, then they turned into the lagoon which made up the public part of Ranworth Broad.

Just as they were about to enter, Sergeant McIver had a further suggestion to make.

" I think it would be best if you kept out of sight, Mr. Rogerson ; if Captain Craven is anywhere about, and is able to see us, we don't want to arouse his suspicions too quickly. If he is led to think that his little deception has worked, he will be all the more likely to make a mistake. If he sees you, he will know that we suspect the truth. If he sees only us, he will think that we are on a routine patrol. If you go into the forward cabin, you can observe a great deal without being seen."

"Good idea! I'll tuck myself away." Hugh went forward, led by the constable. There he was able to keep his eye on the bank through a fairly large porthole.

They cruised slowly round the Broad, moving in a clockwise circle. There was no sign of anything suspicious there, and they moved back again to the entrance channel. On the left-hand side, just where the channel led off towards the mainstream, there could be seen the chain which guarded the entrance to the private section of the Broad. This was wild and overgrown, not having been open to public use for many years. They took a course close to the chain, but they could not see any sign of its having been recently moved or disturbed. "We will take it that nothing has been in there," said Sergeant McIver. "Anyone making use of that stretch of water would immediately draw attention to himself. Besides, that chain does not appear to have been touched for many a long month."

When they came out into the main stream, they turned left and worked steadily round the bend by Ward Marsh, past the Yarmouth Waterworks, and on to the spot where Hugh and John had moored for their first night.

So far, they had had no success. They turned and went carefully back, nosing into one or two inlets, and also turning up the dyke which led to Horning Hall. Eventually they reached the point at which they had begun their search. There they met *Sabrina*, which had been awaiting them. Chris had been busy preparing lunch.

" Any clues ? " called out Mr. Vincent.

" Nothing at all. I'm coming on board again," answered Hugh ; as the launch came alongside, he took a flying leap on to *Sabrina's* deck, prompting a sudden, " Go easy, there ! " from Chris, who had to make a quick move to steady the saucepan which was boiling merrily on the Primus stove in the cooking locker. He was joined, in more sedate fashion, by the sergeant, who had a further discussion with Mr. Vincent.

" There's nothing obvious to be seen ; that's definite," he said. " The only thing is to go over the ground again, more slowly and carefully. Meanwhile I'll signal through to H.Q. again and we'll see if the aeroplanes can do better. I'll tell them not to confuse you with the quarry. I guess she has her mast down, and is well buried among the reeds ; that is, if she is anywhere here at all."

" I can't help thinking that she is," affirmed Mr. Vincent. " Anyhow, we'll begin a slow and steady search ; I presume you will have some reinforcements along soon. Between us, and with the help of the aircraft, we should get some idea."

" All right, sir. I shouldn't advise you to go straight in and tackle her if you find her ; they're ruthless men ; they won't hesitate to shoot if they can see a chance of escape. On the other hand, if we can convince them that they have no chance at all, they will probably come quietly ; they won't want to pile up unnecessary trouble for themselves."

" We'll look out. We'll no doubt see you later."

While the police were moving off, Mr. Vincent suggested a further discussion as they ate lunch.

" Let's think this out from Captain Craven's point of view," he suggested. " He's a clever man, and he's playing for big stakes. He's bound to have had things thoroughly organized. You wouldn't *expect* him to have a hide-out which could be covered in one quick look-round. I guess he's also thought about the possibilities of aerial reconnaissance ; he's no fool. If that's the case, then we can expect the *Windward* to be covered right over in such a way as to make her invisible from any angle."

" Yes, and he would want some kind of entrance to his lair which could be completely

covered over when he was inside," added Hugh.
" I should imagine he would avoid the obvious
places like the small dykes and so on.   How far
back would he have to be in the reeds before he
became invisible from the river ? "

" Something like ten feet, I suppose.   You
can't see very far into them.  It might be possible
to use one of those bushes as top cover, in order to
put aircraft off the scent ; but *Windward* has to
get into the reeds without leaving any trace
behind ; that would not be easy."

" Supposing a whole section of reeds were
planted in a movable bed ?   It sounds fantastic,
I know, but I suppose it *is* possible," said Hugh.
" A wooden frame, filled with mud, could be
planted with reeds, and then used as a kind of
door, and slid in and out of position in order to
let the *Windward* through, and then cover up her
traces.   A channel could be cut into the reed-
bed, and she could there be tucked snugly away.
If it were by one of the bushes or trees, it would
be even more effective.  The channel might
even be cut to lead through to one of the small
patches of open water which are marked on the
map near the mouth of the River Ant."

" Yes, but how can such a hide-out be found,
even if it exists ?   If the aircraft fail to find any
trace of the *Windward*, the general opinion will
be that she has made good her escape.  There is
one of the planes, by the way."

An Auster flew slowly overhead, the observer's

face plainly visible through the perspex window of the cabin. It appeared to be following the course of the river, flying about 100 feet high. They watched it disappear over the treetops, and then continued their discussion as they finished their lunch.

" The only thing, then," suggested Hugh, " would be to hang about here and keep a careful watch in case *Windward* decided to make a dash for it in a few days' time. The chances of getting her like that would be pretty thin."

" They would," said Chris, feelingly. " In any case, let's have a good search round here first—if we go very carefully and slowly, we may yet track her down. Besides, if Hugh's theories are correct, Dick and John are on board, and they may manage to leave some clue about. We have friends on the enemy craft, remember."

They all agreed that some sort of action would in any case be a great relief, and would give them something purposeful with which to fill the afternoon hours, and so they quickly cleared away, and set sail again.

## Chapter 21

### THE UNEXPECTED BECOMES ROUTINE

*SABRINA'S* sails were hoisted again soon after midday ; then began a slow, patient search. It was not made easier by the somewhat gusty wind which continued to blow strongly from the south-west. They put two reefs in the mainsail and one in the jib, but found it awkward work trying to sail slowly along the windward bank of the river. They nosed into the reeds every few yards, probed with the quant pole, peered into the thick clumps of growth, and generally tried to make sure that the ground had been thoroughly covered. Past the end of the dyke which led to Horning Hall they went, and round the U-shaped bend which came after it, but still no suggestion of anything but reeds and marshland.

Overhead, the Auster circled and manœuvred continuously ; soon they ceased to take any notice of its continual droning. Steadily and patiently they persisted in their search, but without any success.

The police launch passed them several times, having been joined by some hired motor-launches ; wireless messages came through at frequent intervals, but there was no news either from the sea-patrols or from the aircraft flying overhead.  The *Windward* had completely disappeared.

By dusk, *Sabrina* had reached the dyke which led to Ranworth Broad.  They turned into it, and moored up near the entrance to the Broad itself ; they were shaded there by the thick cluster of trees which formed part of the ring of trees surrounding the Broad.  They found a firm spot on the bank, and moored up for the night.

The police launch came along again just after they had moored, and stopped to exchange news.  Learning that *Sabrina* had found no clues, the sergeant was quite ready to abandon the search.  He felt that it was obvious that *Windward* had escaped, and that it would be a waste of time to search further.

" I think we ought to maintain wireless contact with you in case we find anything," suggested Hugh.  " You know the wavelength which we use for transmission ; could you listen for us at some agreed time—say eight and ten o'clock tonight, and six and eight o'clock tomorrow morning ?  I presume we shall see you again soon after eight ? "

" Yes ; we shall have to spend at least another day searching ; the Chief is determined to make some headway with this case if he possibly can ; and he's inclined to be very obstinate.  We'll listen for you then ;  eight and ten tonight, six and eight tomorrow."

" Right ;  I think I will transmit *something*,

whether we have news or not ; if you don't hear anything at all, you might come and look us up to see that all is in order."

" Very good ; we're going to moor up at Ranworth staithe for the night ; we wish you well."

" Good night ! "

They spent a quiet evening in *Sabrina's* cabin. Hugh managed to draw Mr. Vincent out a little, and persuaded him to talk about some of his experiences in China during the war years. As he listened to Mr. Vincent's intimate description of China, and of the superstitious fears which overshadow so much of the life of her people, he discovered that another of his pet notions about Christianity was being steadily destroyed.

" I always thought that it was something of a pity to disturb such people's ' simple faith '," he remarked. " It seems that I have been swallowing some more second-hand ideas. I have never heard about the things which you mention ; according to what I had heard, these people live in beautiful, natural simplicity, with a religion that is full of lovely ideas and high principles. This business of awful fear, of evil spirits and dark superstition, is news to me."

" Don't blame yourself too much, Hugh," replied Mr. Vincent. " Others are more to blame than you are. But the fact is that it is absurd to talk about ' improving the conditions '

in which these people live without doing something to change the forces which make those
conditions.    And in every case, you will find
that poverty, dirt, disease and so on can be traced
back, directly or indirectly, to false religion.
You've got to understand rightly the world in
which you live before you can live correctly in
it.    It's their crude, ugly, distorted faiths that
have made their lives ugly and distorted also.
The Gospel of Christ is not a luxury, a sort of
' extra ' which we give to people when we have
given them good drains and good houses.    It's
a necessity.    If you don't get it across to them,
they will as likely as not destroy their houses in
some fierce religious strife (as in India, recently),
or refuse to follow the rules of health because of
some crude superstition. We build hospitals only
as a means to reaching the souls of the people.
Bibles are more important than bridges ! "

Hugh was thoughtful.    " I certainly am learning fast," he remarked.    " I am so glad that we
have met each other, though I would have
wished it to have been in happier circumstances."

Chris interrupted.    " Yes, but you know,
Hugh, God may well have permitted all this to
happen in order to make our meeting possible ;
it may well be that He is using these happenings
to get a message to John and yourself."

Hugh did not feel able to make any immediate
reply.    He was feeling very troubled about

himself and his past attitude to Christianity. He was not yet ready to commit himself, but he had let many of his old ideas go ; he had seen them for what they were—second-hand and often shallow half-truths; cheap sneers, biased opinions.    Like a long-neglected room, into which a shaft of sunlight has suddenly shone, revealing cheap and trashy furniture, his mind was being ruthlessly exposed in the clear light of the Christian witness of his new friends.    What he saw in his own heart was not a pleasing sight ; but it was what he had once accounted true stuff, and he could not throw it out easily.

At about half-past nine, Chris went out into the well to brew cocoa ; as she busied herself there, she began to sing, in her clear, sweet voice ; it was a chorus which Hugh had already discovered to be a family favourite of his new friends.    Her voice sounded above the roaring of the primus :

*Step by step I'll follow Jesus,*
*Hour by hour I'm in His care . . .*
*Day by day He walks beside me,*
*Through the years I'll know He's*
  *there . . . .*

Other choruses followed, as the primus roared away.    Then Chris let the air out of the primus, which gave a last defiant hiss and then subsided into silence.    She repeated the chorus as she stirred the cocoa and prepared the sandwiches for supper.

"*Step by step I'll follow Jesus . . .*"

Hugh had ceased to be surprised, but he still wondered, at the strength of the faith which enabled her to sing so confidently at such a time. Whatever else could be said, there could be no doubt of the reality of the beliefs which meant so much to the Vincents. This was something that made a difference—a worthwhile difference to people.

The singing stopped ; there was a moment's silence.

Suddenly Chris put her face inside the cabin. "Dad ! Hugh ! Come out here quickly ! I thought I heard Dick's voice. Hurry ! Don't make any noise."

Mr. Vincent and Hugh rushed outside into *Sabrina's* well.

Chris spoke in a whisper : " I had brewed the cocoa, and had put my head outside the awning in order to get some water for soaking the saucepan. I was just finishing off the chorus ' Step by step '. When I stopped I heard a faint voice. It sounded just like Dick shouting, ' We're here ! Help ! ' Then it stopped !"

" Good show," said Hugh. " He must have heard your singing and recognized your voice. Let's get searching right away ! I'll get my torch."

" Not so quickly, Hugh, old chap," countered Mr. Vincent. " I suggest that we go below and talk this over before we do anything drastic.

Let's wait a few moments to see if there's anything further to be heard."

They stayed quietly standing on the stern for several minutes, but there was neither light nor sound which would have given them a further clue. They then went below to make further plans.

Mr. Vincent began : " There is a gang of desperate men on that boat ; Sergeant McIver was quite right. Unless we convince them that they haven't a chance, they'll try to fight their way out of trouble. We're not sufficiently armed to cope with them. They don't know for certain that we heard them ; I suggest that we lie low until ten o'clock ; we have arranged to radio the police then. They are moored quite near. If we can get them across to help us, we shall be fairly sure of getting our prey."

" You're right, Mr. Vincent," said Hugh. " There are only ten minutes to go until ten o'clock. We must keep careful watch until then in case they make a dash for it. Have you any idea of the direction from which the sound came, Chris ? "

" Yes, a rough idea ; it was slightly to my left and slightly in front of me. That means they're in the general direction of Ranworth Broad."

" But we had a good look round there in the police boat this morning, and there was no sign of anything ! " said Hugh.

" Yes, but you know you may possibly have

missed something," replied Chris, with gentle sarcasm.

"The whole area is thick with trees and shrubs," said Mr. Vincent. "If there were a passageway through, it would make an ideal hiding-place."

"Anyhow, Chris," Hugh broke in, "you're sure that they were in that direction?"

"As sure as it is possible to be."

"That means that they are on the Ranworth side of us. Would it not be a good idea to swing *Sabrina* across the channel, so that she blocks it and then they won't be able to make a quick getaway while we're waiting to radio the police? Captain Craven's men may also have heard Chris, and will realize that the alarm has been raised."

"That's a good idea, Hugh. We can be doing that right away."

Chris joined Mr. Vincent in the task of untying the stern mooring-rope and swinging *Sabrina* across the width of the channel. They worked as quietly as possible, using the quant pole as a kind of lever, pushing it against the bank in order to avoid splashing noises. It was not completely dark, but the shadow of the trees made that particular stretch of water almost pitch black. *Sabrina* was invisible, except from very close quarters. Anyone coming out of the Broad would have found it almost impossible to see her, since her mast mingled with the background of trees, and her silhouette, apart from the mast, was below the level of the river bank. The wind had almost completely dropped ; only an occasional rustle disturbed the silence. It was an eerie task ; they spoke in whispers, treading softly, striving desperately to avoid making any kind of noise.

The chimes of ancient Ranworth Church rang sweetly out, sounding ten o'clock. Hugh slipped below and turned on the transmitter.

"Hullo, Hullo. *Sabrina* calling. Come at once ; on trail. Urgent."

The reply came quickly : "Message received ; on way. McIver."

Hugh climbed outside again, and reported on the successful contact he had made. Suddenly they heard the throb of the motors of the police launch as it approached them from the opposite side of the Broad.

As the boat drew nearer, their hearts began beating faster with the excitement and new-found hope. There had been no sign of any movement from the *Windward*, if indeed she was nearby ; they could only conclude that she was either lying low, hoping to avoid capture, or else Chris had been deceived by some sound which she had mistaken for Dick's voice. If Captain Craven had decided to lie low, it meant that he was very sure of his lair remaining hidden.

The police launch drew near ; Hugh shone his torch on *Sabrina* in order to make her new

14

position plain, so that the launch would not collide with her in the darkness. The throb of the motors died down, and the black shape of the launch glided silently alongside. Sergeant McIver jumped on board, and went down into the cabin to get the latest news. The position was quickly explained to him. The alternatives were simple enough.

" Either we go right in and begin our search now, thus giving clear warning, or else we wait quietly until morning. If we do the first, there's the risk that *Windward* may escape in the darkness. If we wait, there's no knowing what trickery she may get up to."

" I'm in favour of going in right away," said Mr. Vincent. " We have blocked the exit quite effectively with *Sabrina*, and there isn't much chance of *Windward* being able to outpace your craft. If she does make a dash for it, we shall know by the commotion which she will cause when she runs into *Sabrina*. In any case, it doesn't matter so very much if Craven does get away. You've given a warning to Yarmouth again, I presume ; he'll never get out to sea. And he's not likely to have another hide-away like this. Let's go for him straightaway. There's no telling how long he will be able to keep under control the other elements whom we assume to be on *Windward*."

" It so happens that the local policeman from Ranworth is on board our launch," replied

Sergeant McIver, " and so we are not so badly outnumbered. He was visiting us at the time when your message came through. We may assume that there are five men, at least, and the two ' prisoners '. We should be able to deal with them. I suggest that you leave *Sabrina* here, and join us on the launch."

This was immediately agreed. The police launch swung slowly round, its motors just ticking over ; then, as she pointed in the direction which Chris had indicated, Sergeant McIver switched on the powerful searchlight with which she was equipped. The trees and reeds at the edge of the Broad were lit with a hard, clear light, of peculiarly brilliant whiteness. The concentrated beam reached piercingly into the cluster of trees which came to the very edge of the water at this point.

Slowly the launch edged its way along, the light pivoting backward and forward as the sergeant tried to penetrate deeply into the thick growth. He himself stood behind it, and a little to one side, in case a shot should be fired at the discomfiting source of light.

Round into Ranworth Broad, along the reed-fringed eastern edge, until they reached a point well beyond the range of any voice ; back again, slowly and methodically, and then for some distance along the western side they went. No sign of anything suspicious met their fiercely-concentrated gaze.

" We had better check up on the entrance to the private Broad," said the Sergeant, as they came back to the entrance after their fruitless search in the Broad.    They turned the light full on to the rusty chain which barred the entrance, its centre part so low that it was dipping beneath the surface of the water.    Carefully they surveyed it, but there was every evidence that it had been there undisturbed for many months.  Weeds had grown up from the river bed, and had entangled themselves around it ; these were untouched.    It would have been impossible for a boat to pass through the entrance without having disturbed them.    Once again they paused to take stock of the situation.    While they stood together talking, around the searchlight, Sergeant McIver swung it lazily round the Broad.

" It's strange," he said.    " I really thought that we were on the track this time.    The young lady seems sure enough of what she heard, and it all sounds quite reasonable.    But I rather think that the only thing we can do is to wait until daylight, call in some extra searchers, and give the place a more thorough comb-out."

Just then, the Ranworth constable, who had been watching the searchlight beam as it swung round the Broad, interrupted with :

" Would it be worth while having a closer look at that old half-sunken house-boat, Sergeant ?    It's big enough to get a small yacht inside, if her mast were lowered.    The cabin must have three feet of water in it, and yet there's plenty of headroom, for it was built with such a high roof. If there was some way into it, a small craft could be tucked up quite comfy-like. It would be a rare place for keeping out of sight!"

"But you would have seen them about here beforehand, surely!"

"Come to think of it, I do remember seeing a yacht moored up near to the houseboat during the summer, once or twice. That may have been that other crowd. There's nothing un-lawful about mooring up near to a wreck like that, so no questions would be asked. They could do their dirty work during the darkness."

"Perhaps you're right, Fawcett. Let's go and have a look. We can't do any harm!"

"We'd better have our weapons handy, hadn't we?"

"Yes; but go slowly with them. Once we fire one of those things we shall have hundreds of forms to fill in and reports to make out to explain why we did it."

The launch revved up her engines, started to move in the direction of the wrecked house-boat, and then, having gathered speed, switched off again; the light was turned out, and she glided silently along through the darkness. Slowly she turned, coming up to the house-boat at the end which was most deeply sunken. Suddenly, Ser-geant McIver switched on the light, flooding the wreck with a white beam; he himself went into the bows of the launch, signalled for the engines to be re-started and put into reverse in order to bring her to a standstill, and carefully examined the woodwork at the end of the house-boat cabin. He ran his eye over the whole structure, turned quickly, switched out the searchlight, and returned to the cabin.

" I think we've found something ! " he said in a low, excited tone. " That woodwork has been made into two doors which appear to open outwards. It would be simple enough to sail a yacht straight into the flooded cabin. There are signs of recent finger-marks, too. I think the best thing now is to inform H.Q., and wait until reinforcements arrive. We can send Fawcett in the dinghy to try to collect some help from Ranworth ; our dinghy has an outboard motor, so that we can make use of it for keeping an extra careful watch. There's only one way out, and we can see that that is guarded. Then we can challenge Craven and company with a force which he will not dare to resist."

" I suppose you're right," said Mr. Vincent, " though I don't like leaving the boys in the hands of those men any longer than is necessary."

The police launch began a series of tight circles round the house-boat, her searchlight directed on her all the time. The sharp noise of the little outboard motor on the dinghy split the silence of the night as Constable Fawcett went for help to Ranworth staithe.

Suddenly, whilst the launch was turning round the bows of the house-boat, there was a bright flash, a loud report, and the whole scene disappeared in utter darkness. The searchlight had been shot out by an unseen marksman in the house-boat. At the same time there came the sound of a muffled exhaust from the direction of the wreck ; the fugitive yacht was going to make a further desperate bid for safety.

" Look out !  They're making a dash for it ! " yelled the sergeant.

The motors of the police launch roared into life as she prepared to chase the enemy. *Windward* succeeded in backing out of her lair, and the sound of her exhaust rose as she went full speed ahead for the exit from the Broad. She had no chance of outpacing the police launch, and it seemed that her attempt was doomed to failure.

" Get out of sight, the rest of you," ordered Sergeant McIver.  " They may fire again."

The dim shape of the *Windward* could just be seen as she gathered speed through the water. For the first few moments after the searchlight had been put out, the eyes of those on the police launch had been unable to see anything because of the sudden darkness.  Now they were getting used to it again, and turned to head the enemy off before she could reach the narrow exit.  Her powerful motors roared out as her bows lifted and she began to surge ahead.

Then came the disaster.

From the well of the *Windward* there came a series of staccato reports. A stream of tracer bullets flung themselves at the stern of the launch.

" They've got a tommy gun ! " exclaimed the sergeant. There was a sudden jolting. " What was that ? They've hit the rudder ! I've lost control. I'll have to throttle back."

He was right. A carefully-aimed shot had smashed some vital part of the rudder mechanism, and the launch was heeling violently over as she swung into a sharp turn. She came back to a level keel as the motors were cut off, and slowly swung round in small circles, quite helpless, while *Windward* made straight for the exit.

" We daren't shoot back, for fear of hitting the boys," said Sergeant McIver. " Fawcett has seen the trouble and is coming back, but I rather think the *Windward* will outpace that dinghy easily."

The constable drew alongside, having turned round immediately he heard the first shot. Sergeant McIver and Mr. Vincent jumped on board.

" *Windward* is trying to make a getaway ; chase her as hard as you can ! "

" I'm afraid she's got the legs of us," said the constable. " But we may see in which direction she goes ! "

" You'll do better than that," said Mr. Vincent,

quietly, " You should just be in time to pick up the survivors from the wreck ! "

" What do you mean by that, sir ? "

" Only that *Sabrina* is moored at right angles across the channel there, under the shadow of the trees ; they'll hit her at full speed ! "

" You're right ! I'd forgotten about her. There she goes ! Listen ! And hurry, man, as fast as you can ! "

*Windward* had just turned the corner from the road into the entrance channel. Just as her shadowy outline disappeared from sight there was a heavy crash, a sound of splintering wood, and a shout of surprise. Then followed a moment's silence, and an outburst of excited conversation, mingled with the moans of an injured man.

Sergeant McIver switched on his torch as the dinghy rounded the bend. There they saw a weird scene of confusion and destruction. *Windward* had struck *Sabrina* a glancing blow, for *Sabrina* had apparently turned diagonally across the stream before she was struck. The fugitive had thus been turned from her course, without being greatly slowed down, and had crashed straight into the half-submerged roots of a sturdy overhanging tree. Her bows had been lifted clean out of the water, and had smashed up against a heavy, fallen branch ; her sturdy stem was splintered to matchwood.

" Hands up, all of you ! " ordered Sergeant

McIver, addressing the five men who had gathered in the *Windward's* well. " You can't get away ; you might as well give in. If you have any weapons, the constable here will be glad to relieve you of them."

Fawcett boarded the *Windward*, covered by the sergeant's revolver, and took from the sullen occupants a selection of small weapons, together with the tommy gun which had done the damage to the launch.  Now that they saw themselves to be cornered, the enemy showed no sign of wanting to fight it out further.  They would only risk bringing further punishment on themselves.

" Where are the two boys ? " demanded Sergeant McIver.  " Are they on board ? "

" No ! " replied Captain Craven.

" Then where are they ?  You will pay dearly if anything has happened to them ! "

" Do not worry yourself ; they are quite safe. You will find them on the old houseboat.  We did not want to be bothered with them any further ; they have caused quite enough trouble as it is."

" I hope you're right, for your sake, Captain Craven.  Fawcett, take the dinghy back to the village, and summon help.  Tell Robinson to try to steer the launch with an oar or something ; he should be able to get here, if he takes things carefully.  Mr. Vincent and I will stay on guard here.  And don't forget to rescue those boys ! "

"Very good, sergeant." The dinghy splut-tered, and then roared away into the darkness.

In a very short while the launch had arrived, being steered, somewhat awkwardly, by an oar over the stern, combined with some adroit management of the twin propellers. The pri-soners were transferred to the cabin, and hand-cuffed. In the meantime, the dinghy had returned with two jubilant passengers—Dick and John, none the worse for their adventure. They were greeted with great enthusiasm.

A quick examination showed that *Sabrina* had not suffered serious damage ; the blow struck by the *Windward* had been a glancing one ; the full force of the crash had been taken by the tree on the river-bank. There was a slight dent in her timbers at the point of impact, and some scratches along her varnished side, but she was in perfect order apart from that.

So it was that while the outboard-motor dinghy towed the police launch back to Ranworth staithe, the Vincents, together with Hugh and John, retired thankfully to *Sabrina's* cabin. Ser-geant McIver could now be left to finish off the night's work.

## Chapter 22

### JOHN AND HUGH START A NEW JOURNEY

IT was a much-delayed supper which the occupants of *Sabrina* enjoyed that night. As they sat round the small table in the snug cabin, they compared notes and filled in the gaps in each others' stories.

"You know, I owe Dick an apology," said John, "and now is the time for me to make it. I'm afraid I've had a very low opinion of his intelligence for the past twenty hours or so— ever since he warned Craven that we had made plans to have the alarm raised at four o'clock yesterday morning. At the time, I thought he was crazy, and that he was giving the whole show away. It now seems that he may have saved the situation. What made you do it, Dick? I've never been so mad in all my life."

"Well, John, it was like this. I was figuring things out, and quietly praying for guidance as to the best thing to do. I knew that Chris must have gone to bed very tired that night, and I also knew—I hope she will forgive me— that when she gets to sleep, she needs a bulldozer to move her. I'm afraid that I just doubted whether she would rouse at four."

Chris grimaced, but admitted, quite candidly,

"You were right, Dick; it was a good job you knew me so well."

" I was therefore afraid," Dick continued, "that the alarm would not be raised, perhaps, until six o'clock. But it was obvious that at the speed at which we were moving, and with a favourable tide, we would be through Yarmouth by then. If I had kept quiet, Craven would have carried on and done just that; he might well have succeeded. On the other hand, if I told him that the alarm would certainly be raised at four o'clock he would know that he could not get through Yarmouth by that hour; and it would be useless for him to try once a watch had been posted; for one thing, there are two bridges to be negotiated. I hesitated, prayed about it again, and felt definitely that I should speak. I had no idea what he would do if he did change his plans, but anything was better than being taken out to sea. So I spoke up, as you heard, John. I shall never forget the look upon your face as I did it ! "

" I felt even worse than I looked, I can assure you. But it certainly seems that you prevented a disaster. We guessed that something had gone wrong when the *Windward* began to slow down, and then stopped, without our having felt anything of the rocking or swaying that we should have done if we had gone out to sea. The other chaps on board seemed to be very het up, especially the three foreigners, and Captain

Craven had quite a job trying to keep them from taking control forcibly. He argued with them, however, and they had to admit in the end that he was right. But their looks were black as night—though even then they were not so bad as they were after you shouted through the port-hole ! ''

" No ; they could quite easily have brained me then ! I wonder they didn't. I hesitated about doing it, for that reason. I'd recognize that charming voice of Chris's anywhere '' (he grinned at his sister as he said this), " and when I heard her singing, I guessed that we must be somewhere in the Broads area, and that by some wonderful providence *Sabrina* was quite near. The guard had become a little slack—they seemed to be very confident that their lair would not be discovered—and so I managed to move round so that my head was near a porthole. Then, just after Chris had stopped singing, I saw a brief opportunity, took a deep breath, opened the porthole before they could get at me, and shouted with all my strength.''

" They jumped on you like tigers on their prey,'' observed John, " and they would have reduced you to pulp if Craven had not come in immediately on hearing the shout. He was furious enough, but he could see that if they were to be discovered (and there was still good hope of escape) they did not want to have any further crimes laid to their charge. I don't think they were quite sure whether your shout was a sort of despairing effort, a ' shot in the dark ', or whether you really had some definite reason for shouting just then. Anyhow, it did the trick, and here we are, safe and sound, and very far from where we might have been."

" Yes, it's been an exciting couple of days," observed Mr. Vincent. " We little thought, when we first met, that we should so swiftly be plunged into a first-class adventure. We came here for a restful holiday. I rather think that we need it even more than we *did*, after all this excitement ! "

" I can't say that I feel particularly done in," added John. " But if I may speak for myself, I feel that I've got something more out of this business than a string of exciting memories."

"Yes," said Mr. Vincent, encouragingly. "What is that ? "

" I've had some shocks of a deeper kind— and of a much more important kind, too. I had something of a shake-up during my summer holidays, as I have told Dick here ; I ran into a crowd of chaps who obviously had had a very true and deep experience of the power of Christ. They made me feel that I was missing something. But I had not gone any further into the subject until we met you. Since then, I've seen that you three share the same wonderful secret ; and by the way you live, and also by some of the things you have said, I have been deeply impressed. I want

to know more.   I realize that I have been blindly
swallowing other people's opinions, and that it is
time that I really thought about things for
myself."

" It looks as if you and I are in the same boat
—in more than one sense," said Hugh, taking
up the theme.   " I've had a couple of very
interesting and helpful discussions with Mr.
Vincent and with Chris here, and I must make the
same confession as you have done.   All this has
been like the discovery of a new world to me.
I have always written religious people off as
being stuffy, narrow-minded, timid, afraid to face
facts, and so on.   I've considered that people
like H. G. Wells and Co. were the true leaders
of modern thought.   I admired them for what I
thought was their freedom from old ideas and
traditions.   Now I discover that they themselves
are as narrow in their outlook, and as afraid of
facing the facts, as anybody else.   What's more,
they certainly haven't the power to change and
inspire folk in the way that Christ does.   You,
Dick, and Chris, and your father—you obviously
have something living and real ; perhaps you
would say that it should be described as ' Somebody ' : the thing is, I know that I haven't, and I
also want to know more."

Mr. Vincent nodded sympathetically.

" I think it would be wise to close down for
this evening," he said.   " We've all had a very
hectic time.   We have some ten days in front of

us, and we shall have plenty of opportunity to thrash these things out together.

" John and Hugh, I need not say how glad we are to hear what you have just said. We will do our best, with God's help, to clear up any difficulties that remain. I believe that the Lord Himself has brought us together in this remarkable way, in order that we might help you to know Him. I have seen Him using more surprising methods even than this. When He sets His love upon someone, He follows him down many a long and unexpected way, but He will find him in the end. I think He is very near to you both. I suggest we have prayers now, and then turn in."

The others nodded agreement ; they were all feeling the strain of the hours of excitement and danger through which they had so recently passed.

Mr. Vincent opened his Bible. He turned to the end of St. John's Gospel, and began to read the verses which speak of Thomas's unbelief, and the way in which it was answered. The majestic yet simple words came with tremendous power in the quiet of the cabin.

" ' Then came Jesus, the doors being shut, and stood in the midst, and said, Peace be unto you.

' Then said He to Thomas, Reach hither thy finger, and behold My hands (" Marked with the scars of the Cross," commented Mr. Vincent) and reach hither thy hand and thrust it into My side (" Where the soldier's sword had pierced Him ") : and be 'not faithless, but believing.'

" It was the Risen Lord, you will notice ; but He directed Thomas's attention to the marks of His death. That is how He first comes to us. He is a Living Master and Friend, but we can only begin to know Him as we realize that our sins had a part in His Death, and that His offering of Himself in our place is our only hope of forgiveness in God's sight. We meet Him as a Saviour Who died ; we may then go on to know Him as a Lord Who lives and reigns."

Mr. Vincent continued the reading :

" ' And Thomas answered and said unto Him, My Lord and my God.'

" That," added Mr. Vincent, in his quiet but musical voice, " is how He still receives us. We will spend a few moments in prayer."

They bowed their heads as he led them into the Presence of God. In simple words he put himself in the place of John and Hugh, and spoke in such a way that they could echo his prayer, and make it their very own. When he had finished, having added a word of deep thanksgiving for the way in which they had been spared, there came a sincere and fervent " Amen " from each of those present.

There was a moment's silence. Then John's voice was heard. It was an unusual kind of voice for John ; trembling slightly, hesitant, charged with emotion, yet well under control :

" O God ; You know how I have ignored and disobeyed You many times ; You know that I don't deserve anything from You but to be left to go on my own foolish way. But I thank You for bringing me here, and for showing me what a mess I was making of running my own life. I cannot wait any longer ; there are many things which puzzle me still, but I have seen the one thing that matters : that Christ loved me and died for me. I ask You to accept me now, and make Him so real to me that I may love and serve Him all my life."

Hugh remained silent ; but the " Amen " with which he had echoed John's prayer said enough to make the hearts of the Vincent family overflow with joy.

*THE END*